Time & Tide

a screenplay by

P. A. Fitzgerald

Time and Tide
ISBN 978-0-6456581-7-0
First published 2023

Cover design by
Graham Davidson
Typesetting by Rack and Rune Publishing
https://rackandrune.com

RACK & RUNE
publishing

Time and Tide

Time and Tide

#1   EXT. RURAL DANISH VILLAGE GARDEN 1819 – DAY
Open on a beautiful garden. Long grass, apple trees, daffodils and
jonquils resemble a 19th century Scandinavian landscape painting by LARSEN. In a far corner, a wooden shed, bleached grey by
long hard winters, hunkers down, as if rooted to the earth. Nearby, NILS SALSTROM (10, wiry and fair-haired), "is" a statue
sitting in an antique outdoors chair cradling a violin.

A Chopin piano lesson suddenly emanates from an upstairs window of the tall gabled house behind him. The boy gazes at cows
grazing in the adjacent meadow and the pine forest that frames it.
This "still life" scene animates slowly as the boy coaxes astonish-
ing music from the instrument. He turns his face to the house for
a moment, as the piano-student audibly falters.

CUT TO ANOTHER ANGLE. Suddenly the tranquil ambience dissolves. NILS is now seen from the POV of a large threatening figure draped in brown, and partly concealed in a grove of silver birch fringing the garden. NILS jumps from his chair in shock as a branch breaks nearby. He stares at a looming hairy brute in high collared great-coat and a tricorn hat, standing half hidden among the trees.

MAN(DANISH& SUB TITLES)

You! Boy! Are you the brat of that rutting
goat SALSTROM?

NILS (HE CAN BARELY SPEAK)

Jeg hedder..jeg hedder NILS..

When he re-opens his eyes the man's melted back into the wood-land.

LARS SALSTROM

NILS! Mother needs her medicine. Come
now please son.

But NILS' legs are "cemented" to the spot and the image "freezes".
The garden's now a dangerous place
SUPER TASMANIA, AUSTRALIA PRESENT DAY 2027

#2 EXT. TASMANIAN MOUNTAIN FOREST - AUTUMN
DAY

Lowering morning mists, blanket the mountain hollows. Lush
bush and a host of ghost gums loom more distinctly as the day
brightens. PAN TO God's eye POV through trees to valleys,
snow-capped hills, mountains and endless forest: it's another
Eden.

#3 SLOWMO - PANNING POV OF THIS PARADISE.

Peace is jolted abruptly by the thudding of something heavy
crashing through the undergrowth, The wraith-like figure of a
man suddenly erupts out of mists shrouding a dense stand of can-
dlestick gums. He's athletic, and running too fast for a close view,
but he might be Nordic.
He half turns his face to see a huge razorback boar is gaining on
him as he sprints towards a seven metre wide cleft in the moun-
tainous terrain spanning a fifty metre drop to jagged rocks. He
clears it like an Olympic long jumper despite wearing a small
back pack, and rolls after landing. The monster pulls up suddenly.
It's more than a half ton of malevolence and watching the man,
ALEX SELKIRK (Maybe 45 And handsome in a slightly grizzled
way).

> ALEX (RASBERRY-ING THE BOAR)
> Faen! No foxes, no feral porkers on this
> island, they said! Stupid country! All the
> creatures just want to eat you or poison you.

He now disappears into thinning mist before re-emerging in forest a hundred metres away. PAN TO
Atop a hillock, staring down at an idyllic glade and gurgling

brook, he briefly succumbs to a bizarre catatonic trance. In the trance he recognizes something. DISSOLVE TO:

#4 EXT. ZAGROS MOUNTAIN GLADE MESOPOTAMIA. DAY. 1847 4

Like a persistence of vision there's a similar glade in another mountain forest. His memory images is surreal, suggesting it's in the distant past. A lion emerges from the forest and drinks from this other brook. DISSOLVE TO:
SEMI PHOTOGRAPHIC ANIMATION: In "flashback" a well-built, sandy hair and bearded Dane, NILS SALSTROM (late 30's), is wearing a bloodied French Foreign Legion uniform, when he staggers out of woodland into the glade. A long-barrelled pistol is in his belt, a sabre in his scabbard.
A closer view is startling, because of his stunning resemblance to a much younger version of ALEX, the runner in the mountains. In 1847 NILS fires his pistol in the air and the lion bounds off into the woods. He abruptly starts a hacking cough and collapses to his knees near the brook, as if he's dying.
A shaft of sunlight strikes a small island in the stream. From NILS' POV the tiny island is blanketed with small ferns and exotic plants. A closer glimpse of this younger bearded face proves conclusively that ALEX and NILS are the same person. ALEX has somehow survived 200 years! DISSOLVE TO

#5 EXT DAY. TASMANIAN MOUNTAIN FOREST GLADE. PRESENT 5

Back in 2027, ALEX's body shudders epileptically as he comes out of the trance. He's unaware of his fit as he trots down towards the brook and veers off the path. He drops out of sight when he enters a copse of ferns. CLOSE He clutches a very old pained illustration of plants as he searches. DISSOLVE TO
LAUNCESTON AND HOBART (FILMIC COMBINATION OF BOTH CITIES)ALEX, SITS IN AN OUTSIDE café READING THE HOBART MERCURY.It's soon apparent he is watching a middle aged woman who Slightly resembles him.

#6 EXT. GROUNDS OF WICOW HIGH SCHOOL. PRESENT DAY 6

Tepid sunlight creeps over a grey black sky. There's a sound wall of torrential rain and howling wind. A tree-fringed school football field surrounded by an ugly encroaching suburban landscape takes shape. The River Derwent flows like treacle in the background.

Pale sunlight grows and the indistinct figure of a man carrying a large black case starts to materialize. It's elemental, mythic even, as he trudges into the foreground, buffeted by powerful winds, before pausing in the deluge. It's easy to get the feeling he might be the harbinger of change. In the distance the wail of a siren can be heard.

The man stares at a mixture of grim forbidding Dickensian buildings and the ugly and vandalized fifties era concrete "pillar box" classrooms and at the metallic sign name WICKLOW HIGH SCHOOL which looms large..

Time seems out of sync as he battles towards the Administration office. It's finally recognizable as being ALEX (BORN NILS SALSTROM), in long black raincoat and carrying a waterproof guitar case. CLOSE His rain-spattered face is a map: he's seen it all. He stops at a building where the walkway diverges.

#7 INT/EXT.YEAR 10 CLASSROOM WICKLOW HIGH – 2027 NOW DAY.

At period break, SALLY (15, sad faced, shy and pretty) and her friend GRETEL (15, Juno-esque, sweet, self-conscious, bitterly unhappy) are being mocked by three cruel and extremely nasty girls. Raelene, the bullies' leader (16, solid, strident punk, make-up like armour) is a nightmare. But maybe a victim too?

RAELENE
Y'ous are nothin' but skanky ho's. Dykes and
Lesos! And teachers' pets.

Nearby, GRETEL's brother DAMIEN (14), pale, slight, fearful sits with lowered head, squirming. Two man-sized thuggish lads,

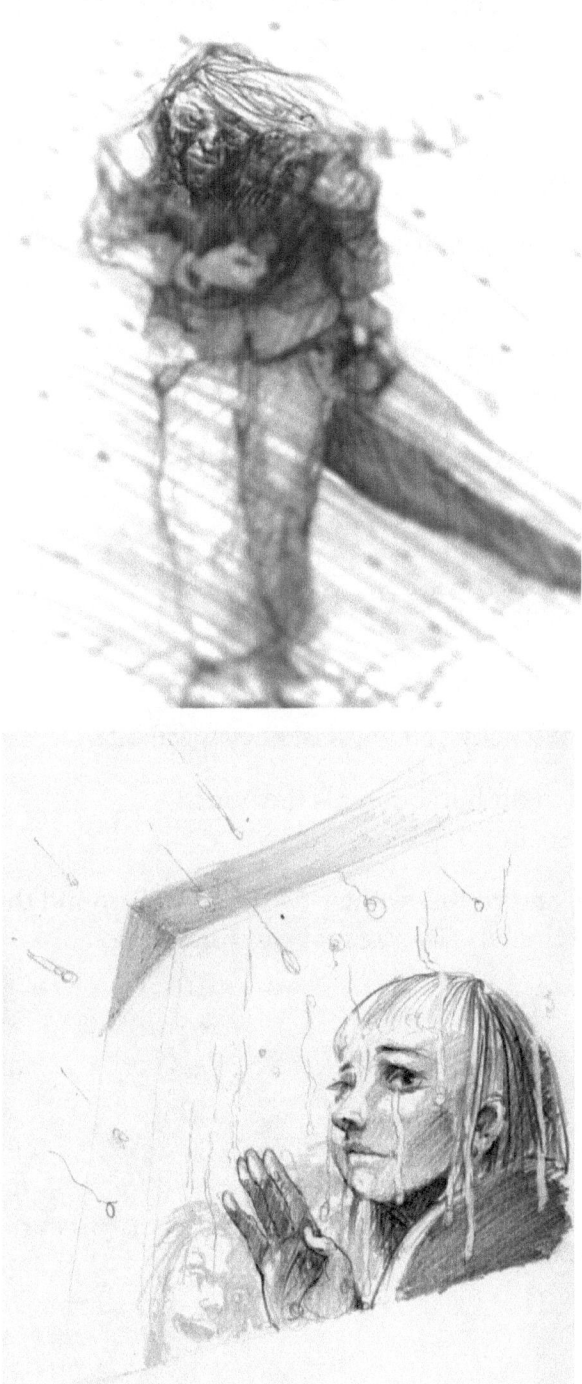

CHAD and WAYNE, are similarly tormenting him. Their friend MARTY looks uncomfortable.

CHAD
Hey Gay boy.. who said you could sit there?
That seat's not for girls.

He kicks the chair so it whacks into DAMIEN'S leg.

WAYNE
You BETTER have done my fuckin' Maths
homework DAMIEN. I mean it.

DAMIEN hands him some neatly written pages.

DAMIEN
Y yeah, got all ththe Alegebraic Equations d
done WWW WAYNE.

WAYNE(EVIL BUT SMART)
Wwucky you wwwaskelwy wwabbit.

(He makes to hit him but pulls the punch).
So..nothing today! Enjoy!

RAELENE and co follow their two 'victims" around the room, their words bullets. They're really intimidating.

The victims "fold into themselves" clutch hands and sidle towards the windows. As they peer out at ALEX, from his POV the rivulets of rain on the window "seem to cry for them". But he waves cheerfully and they do the same. Their eyes follow him as he heads towards the General office.

#8 INT. SCHOOL ADMINISTRATION OFFICE – MODERN DAY

In a small bright room adjacent to the Admin office, JESS,(slim, stylish blonde mid 20's) looks up from the photocopier as ALEX is seemingly "blown in" through though the powerful doors. It's almost Gothic. Secretary DOREEN (fashion tragic 55 going on 25), glances at the handsome Civil War era gentleman on the cover of the "Gone with the Wind" prequel "RHETT" on her desk and then at ALEX. They look alike. Her face softens as she smells his abnormally strong pheromones. JEN's curious and comes to the counter.

> DOREEN
>
> It's all good, Mister Selkirk, er ALEX. Except - there's a mistake on your listed age. It says 63?

> ALEX
>
> Mistake? No. No mistake.

> DOREEN
>
> Really - yy? Um, well, in that case, welcome to Wicklow High. I, hope you stay longer than the last Music Teacher did. And I'm sorry to be the bearer of bad news, but you have to teach a bit of History as well till they can find a specialist. I'll let the Head know you've arrived. Actually he's a bit more than a Head. He'll see you soon.

The women share a silly sense of humour and laugh.

> JESS
>
> Hello there. JENNIFER RYAN. Everybody calls me JENN.

She too smells the pheromones and is affected.

> ALEX
>
> Ahuh! ALEX.

> JESS
>
> You can get a decent coffee in the brown
> room down that corridor. And a piece of my
> birthday cake too. But don't ask.

Alex nods "thanks" and heads off down the corridor.

> DOREEN
>
> Back off SCARLET! RHETT's mine. He said
> 63 remember! Anyhoo, I saw him first.

> JESS
>
> More like RHETT-ched. Get a life Doreen -
> he's a grumpy old man. He did smell alright
> though. I'll absolutely have to get some of
> that aftershave for JASON.

JESS heads back to the duplicating room grinning. From their POV Headmaster CARL FROBISHER sticks his head out the door (50, short, balding, expensive suit) as he clearly doesn't like their risque conversation.

#9 INT. HALLWAY AND MUSIC ROOM - NEXT MORNING

ALEX strolls along the gloomy maze-like corridors of an ugly late 1800's building wing towards his first class.
O/S POV He stops abruptly in disbelief as a couple of hulking seniors disguised in bikers' skull faced wind masks lurk near a building across the asphalt yard, openly drinking beer from a long neck. Alex looks for an exit door but they're too far away to catch, and gesture crudely when they see him watching and run off into a nearby building.

#10 INT. MUSIC ROOM. WICKLOW – DAY 2027

O/S POV FROM ALEX'S POV MUSIC ROOM is written in large red letters on a wooden door ALEX silently opens and he's instantly assailed by a wall of sound.

GRETEL, SALLY and DAMIEN look apprehensive as ALEX walks to the teacher's desk. MARTY (solid, sullen, sports jock) watches their eyes and also notes Alex's intensity and physicality. Most of the other 30 odd 14-16 year-olds in the room are oblivious to ALEX. Damien watches English Mistress ROWENA (50) stop as she's passing, and peer in. She's clearly once been a looker but has let herself go. Her face shows she thinks ALEX's task hopeless.

CLOSE ON ALEX hooking up his leads and cables to an instrument machine with music he's pre-recorded.

ALEX (HALF ALOUD)
Hip bone's connected to the neck bone, head
bone's connected to the wish bone.

He misses nothing that's happening in the room though. Lead-plugging complete, he attaches amplifiers and strums.

FROM ALEX'S POV Two not-so-bright overgrown Home Boy types are wrestling. He notes a semi concealed knife under the shirt of one of these thugs and his face hardens. He also notes two "Barbie doll" girls and a feral obese boy laughing at a pornographic magazine.

ECU ON ALEX's fingers lingering on the amp switch. He's livid as he watches Raelene and harpy cronies JEANNIE and CHERYL leaning over GRETEL and SALLY, threatening them. JEANNIE tweaks GRETEL's nipple and she cries out. ALEX grits his teeth. Most students now intuit ALEX's mood and truculently sit and watch him with defiant looks.

ALEX jacks the plug into the amp, and it's an equivalent impact to letting off a hand grenade as he breaks into booming renditions of classic Australian rock. The kids are transfixed, disbelieving as he plays and sings a brilliant "bracket". The bullies' faces register mounting alarm.

> ### ALEX
> No points if you answered Hip Hop, Seattle
> Grunge or elevator music. By Christmas
> you'll be playing some of this stuff. All
> things being equal, you'll also be able to tell
> LISZT from Listerine, RAVEL from Reveille
> and BOCCELLI from Bolognese.
>
> (Aside) But even shite from shoe polish'd be
> a good start.

DISSOLVE TO MOVING: ALEX plays loudly, strolling around the room. He already "knows them". His physicality and charisma send a clear message. As the bell rings, he nods to the seven bullies to stay and a head flick at the door dismisses the rest. He waits in the doorway as each bully file out, speaking two words to each in turn. The last boy squirms when ALEX holds out his hand for the knife.

> ### ALEX
> Uh uh! This is a Police matter now JACK!
> Unless you swear right here, on your oath,

ALEX

you won't ever carry again...it's a one-time
offer.

JACK

I swear I won't. Thanks sir.

The shocked youth hurries out nodding gratefully.

#11 INT. MUSIC ROOM – DAY

JOANNA (15, cluey class comedienne, sweet Goth) returns to the
room and gives him an "I'm an out there crazy just like you" look,
and places a sandwich on his desk.

JOANNA(MAYBE HAS A CRUSH)

I forgot to give you some little lunch Sir. That
was a choice lesson Mister.. um..! Sure beats
the crap out've singin' "Advance Australia
Fair" till yer puke!

ALEX

Not a flag waving patriot, eh JOANNA?

JOANNA
How come you know my name sir?

After she closes the door on him, he briefly buckles over in a coughing spasm before heading off to another class.

#12 INT. HISTORY CLASSROOM - DAY.

He's late and unwell to the senior class: they're a mixed bag - two fringe sociopaths, the rest mainly "Ferals", the chronically bored and a couple of quiet serious students. An old projector is prepped. One window has broken Venetian blinds, but the day's dark enough to screen films. CCU the lesson notes on the desk are about "The Peoples of Mesopotamia". He's bemused.

ALEX
Erm, good morning Year 11. I'm the late Mr Selkirk (Glancing at a wall clock) I'm your substitute today.

GABE
Where's Ms KANDINSKY sir?

ALEX
With a name like that? Um, maybe painting
the town..I think she might be at an In
Service course

JAYDEN
Whatever the fuck that is..

KYLIE
It means she's taken a Sickie - or having a
pregnancy test, Dipshit.

ALEX
Okay enough.. "cussing" and speculative
fiction. Um, today we'll be looking at the
Sumerians Babylonians and Assyrians. And by
looking, I mean that your teacher's found this
ancient film of these very ancient civilizations
located in what's now Iraq and Turkey. Luckily,
I actually know something about this subject.

JARROD
How's come? Were you there mate?

There's general laughter at the class clown.

ALEX
As a matter of fact I was, Mr Clever Clogs.

They know Teachers are eccentrics and let it pass).
Anyway, this old doco film is a smart
amalgam of two way-old films: the first is a
Silent movie called "Intolerance"

21

ALEX

made by the great DW GRIFFITHS with the
entire peasant class population of Mexico
as extras by the looks of it...nearly 100 years
ago. The other's a BBC narrated film about
the Epic of GILGAMESH, the hero of the
oldest ever recorded story

JARROD(A LIKEABLE ROGUE)

So did you meet this wanker GOLLYGOSH
or GLOWMESH or what's his face, when
you were over there Sir?

ALEX

Course I did! Taught him how to play
Stairway to Heaven on guitar and all. So
write down any questions as they come to
mind - we'll discuss when it's finished.

There's groaning and swearing. ALEX is sick and slumps into a
corner seat at the back of the room. The projector whirs. The rare
footage of these ancient lands stirs imaginations. The Screen POV
pans along the ancient walls of URUK. Bronze armoured soldiers
patrol the walls. A chariot driven by a fierce warrior with plaited
hair and beard emerges from the city through the giant cedar city
gates.

JARROD

That bloke looks like a Hippie on dinosaur
steroids Mr SELKIRK.

Alex is in a bad way at the back

NARRATOR(PRETENTIOUS BBC VOICE)

..and thus, after the death of his only worthy
adversary and friend ENKIDU, the warrior
king GILGAMESH set a northern course

through Mesopotamia on his Great quest in
search of the fabled elixir of youth, a plant
with magical properties...

CLOSE: Alex slumps in his seat but the film's noisy so he's unnoticed staring at the flickering images and into oblivion. FADE TO BLACK:

#13 SUPER - M E S O P O T A M IA 1847 A.D.

EXT. DESERT region. IRAQ - DAY

Blanket darkness yields to sunlight in an eclipse-like DISSOLVE. Sand blows like waves over a timeless landscape. In a moment of déjà vu - a familiar soldier materializes from a small dust storm.. The man leading the foot soldiers is NILS SALSTROM. He looks to be more than 20 years younger than he does as ALEX, the teacher in modern 2011 Hobart, and handsome despite evident world weariness. His Foreign Legion uniform's stained with blood and he wears knee length leather boots and a kepi on his head with a white neck flap attached. Wraith-like, he disappears and reappears in the sandstorm reminiscent of the way he does in the mists of the opening scenes.

Gradually, behind him, a rag tag "army" of perhaps 200 European, Turk, Arab and Persian mercenaries, emerge from whirling dust. CAPTAIN MUSTAPHA, (large and pompous Turkish officer), canters to the head of the column on a magnificent Arab stallion.

FROM THE POV OF A HIGH FLYING DOVE: the foot soldiers are a winding column, shuffling towards a palm-flanked Euphrates several miles distant. Many are bloodied and bandaged. NILS smiles as the Captain canters past the column like a Mediaeval potentate inspecting his "mighty horde".

NILS (HALF AUDIBLE)
Ever your humble servant your Ottoman-
ship... of the desert.

NILS draws his pistol and waits as two struggling stretcher bear-
ers carrying a dying BERBER, appear.

NILS
He's suffered enough! Lay him on the sand
yonder. Time for an end to pain OMAR. I
hope it's to a better place you go. ALLAH
Akbar!

The soldiers' faces register no emotion as the loud report of his
pistol is heard.. DISSOLVE TO

#14 INT. CLASSROOM PRESENT DAY. 2027   14

Most of the class are strangely interested in the film. A lone
academic female glances back at ALEX but the room grows even
darker as another thunderstorm blackens the sky.

MARION
This is actually interesting Sir. And isn't it
strange this is the same place that Oscar
winning film "The Hurt Locker" was set.
And that our soldiers were fighting there too
till recently. It all looked so amazing back
then..

The other students really listen to her and from her POV ALEX
seems to be watching the film. CLOSE. ALEX's eyes flicker in
"R.E.M mode", with the flickering film. For a moment he watches
the "shuttering" SILENT, as hordes attack the Hanging Gardens
of Babylon, before seeing the images of his past once again.

#15 EXT.MESOPOTAMIA NEAR URUK 1847.DAY.

The mercenaries set up tents near ancient ruins. Nils walks out of
sight of his men and coughs up blood. He leans against a broken

fortress rampart skimming pages of a book titled "Cities of Antiquity: Legendary; Mythical; Real! He regards the Pen and ink drawings of URUK and curiously glances at nearby ruins.
DISSOLVE TO

#16A EXT. MESOPOTAMIA. ENCAMPMENT. DUSK

At dusk NILS strolls through the encampment. Many soldiers are on their knees facing Mecca. Drawn by the sound of a mandolin, NILS listens rapt to a young Italian playing inexpertly to a grateful audience.

FRANCESCO
You are familiar with this piccolo Strumento Lieutenant? Try make better noise than GIORGIO!

FROM THE SOLDIERS' POVS NILS is shy and almost scared to touch the instrument but relents and plays. They're gob-smacked at his skill, but he stops abruptly.

NILS
I'm sorry. Too many years....

His voice fades and he wanders away visibly affected.

#16B EXT. CAMPFIRE NEAR URUK 1847. NIGHT.

GIORGIO
Something terrible must have happen to that man. He look like he dead already.

CORPORAL LEES
Ay, a lost soul indeed.

SOUND DISSOLVE TO - shovels digging into hard sand.

#17 EXT. DESERT NEAR URUK RUINS 1847 – DAY

Two BERBERS dig a grave. Between them and the Euphrates, camp is being broken. NILS finishes writing a diary entry and he and beefy CORPORAL LEES spell them. LEES digs first. He's slow and unfit, so Nils takes his place.

From NILS'POV The Corporal dozes off on the sand. A metre down NILS is stunned when his shovel strikes something. He carefully pulls a magnum sized object wrapped in rotted linen from the damp sand. He peels the linen and finds a mummified hand clutching a priceless ruby and emerald-encrusted golden dagger.

NILS (WHISPERED)
Oh my God! A king's ransom!

He greedily hides the object in his jacket's deep pocket and digs with renewed energy. Once he glances south, desertion on his mind but again he strikes something.

CORPORAL(WAKING IN SHOCK)
Oh JESUS! What were tha' sound!

Together, they haul from the hole the fierce stone bust of a sneering ancient king.

NILS(SPREADS ARMS THEATRICALLY)

My name is OZYMANDIAS, King of Kings. No, more likely in these parts..my name is GILGAMESH, King of URUK. Look on my works ye mighty and despair. Apologies to the dead poet SHELLEY.

NILS is socially inept, suddenly aware he's not alone here.

All the great Museums of Europe would covet this Corporal. This bust may even be that hero king. It's said his strength was such he killed lions with his bare hands, thousands of years before Christ, and feared nothing, but..

CORPORAL LEES

But what sir?

NILS

His own mortality. The story says he found the legendary plant that was the first Fountain of Youth, though only briefly.

CORPORAL LEES

I could'na imagine somethin lonelier than endurin' youth, lest them as near'n dear t'me had that selfsame gift.

NILS (ALEX)gives him a "so, still waters" do "run deep" look, then projectile vomits blood, and falls to his knees. LEES hands him a vial of pinkish liquid.

CORPORAL

It cannot cure yer Consumption Sir but can 'elp with pain.'It's Laudenum' ey got from a Chinee in DAMASCUS.

Might give you hallucinations, but 'tis a
small price to pay fer sleep.

#18 EXT. NEAR URUK - DUSK. FLASHBACK 1847

NILS is "stoned", wandering among the ruins, holding his antiquarian book, patting the golden dagger. He holds up the drawing
of this ruined city: it shows the great cedar gate, battlements, tur-
rets. His vision's blurred but for seconds the stones seem real - it's
the blurring of his flashback "vision" and "ALEX's" semi conscious
view of the film his class watches in the classroom. DISSOLVE
TO

#19 INT/EXT.HISTORY ROOM AND ANCIENT MESOPO-
TAMIA

Present and past coalesce: it's visually ambiguous. ALEX half consciously watches Ancient URUK and its denizens on the screen,
and his flashback memory of that place in the past, suddenly blur.
DISSOLVE Again the two eras coalesce.
FROM NILS' POV: The documentary film URUK "on" the screen
and URUK in his memory vision alternately surge and fade,
and the gathering sunlight and classroom darkness vacillate like
shuttering night and day". On screen, two SUMERIAN boys stop
a stick-sword fight as they hear horses whinnying. Desert winds
blow loudly as two times coincide. In 1847 Nils closes his eyes
and spreads his arms to the elements.

NILS (WHISPERED)
What in Christ's name...!

#20 INT. MESOPOTAMIA FLASHBACK.1847 -DREAM
NIGHT.

CLOSE ON NILS asleep in his tent.
O/S POV In a dream NILS stands near a 19th century European
church looking at a tiny hillock with a gnarled and eerie solitary
tree, its weeping branches stooping over a single cross and grave-
stone. It's haunting and he forcibly wakes himself. DISSOLVE TO:

#21 EXT. ZAGROS MOUNTAINS FOOTHILLS – 1847 DAY

NILS seems ready to desert as he watches his comrades through
a telescope from the crook in a tree 5 miles away, but when he
sights scores of robed Bandits through the telescope heading
towards his Unit,his conscience wins out and he gallops off after
them.

#22 EXT. ZAGROS MOUNTAINS 1847.

THE MERCENARIES LOOK MUTINOUS AS THE
CAPTAIN LEADS THEM INTO THE DANGEROUS RISING
FOOTHILLS.

GEORGIO

So..our brave DANISH Lieutenant, no one
speziale. Desert us, just like any other man.

CORPORAL

He must 'ave his reasons GIORGIO, fer he
were a good man, but not long fer this world

GEORGIO looks surprised at this. Suddenly mounted snipers fire
sporadically at the column, before cantering into the foothills.
Two Mercenaries fall dead.

#23 ZAGROS MOUNTAINS 1847

PANNING THROUGH HIS TELESCOPE, NILS' POV
Shots bring down more Mercenaries. They look ready to mutiny.

#24 MOUNTAIN FOOTHILLS - LATER THAT DAY

The mercenaries traipse along a rising mountain gorge unaware
of the growing numbers waiting in ambush. Shots ring out and
the captain falls dead a moment before the bandit sniper lands
dead just ahead of the column. At this moment Nils gallops up to
them.

NILS (TURKISH)
Ru--uuuun! Run For your lives

It's too late. Bandits arrive in unbeatable numbers, many on horseback. All mercenaries are butchered bar NILS(ALEX) and three agile young Persians. NILS is a fierce fighter and kills half a dozen with sword and pistol before running and scaling the dangerous heights like a mountain goat.

#25 EXT. ZAGROS MOUNTAIN HEIGHTS - NEAR DUSK

He climbs frantically and reaches a long cliff top plateau and an impossible climb above that. A group of the BANDITS on horseback have followed him to the mountain top along a perilous trail. He spies the dust cloud of his pursuers' horses a half mile away and runs along the awesome cliff top looking for a miracle. FLASH BACK

#26 INT. HISTORY CLASSROOM PRESENT DAY.2027

Back in the classroom the film shows a sunrise in this same area 4500 years earlier. GILGAMESH follows cuneiform markings on a cliff wall til he reaches a cave mouth. He calls until a wiry, ancient man emerges from the darkness and recognizes him. It has a modern sound track and BBC narration overlaying the Silent films but the original sub titles remain. Class clown JARROD mutes the sound with the remote and reads the sub titles in a passable ANTHONY HOPKINS' HANNIBAL LECTOR voice. It's spooky. Most are impressed but some uncomfortable as it's like he's channelling a spirit.

> ### UTNAPISHTIM (JARROD'S VOICE)
> UTNAPISHTIM am I, survivor of the Great
> Flood, and twelve hundred blazing summers.
> It is known to me you have crossed the
> Ocean of Death, now a desert, and I above
> all others know what it is you seek, son of
> LUGALBANDA, King of the Sumerians. In
> the
>
> language before time, the ancients called it
> the Flower of Born Again.
>
> Once it sheltered at the bottom of the sea but
> in these times hides in other secret places. So
> mark you now, where the tree-line meets the
> melting snow streams there is a glade, and
> in that glade a fern with blue green berries.
> When you see it you will know it, for it is
> loved by the islands in streams, by filtered
> sunlight, and by isolation.

MOVING In a similar scene to that of Alex in the Tasmanian woods, Gilgamesh ghosts through the mists of the alpine forest. He suddenly spies a unique fern-like plant growing on a tiny island in a stream. A shaft of sunlight strikes it as the sky clouds over.

#27 EXT.URUK MESOPOTAMIA 1847 DAY.FLASHBACK MEMORY

NILS (ALEX) races along the cliff face pursued by the murderous band, glancing over the edge as he runs and sights a sturdy little bush clinging obstinately to the face of the escarpment two

metres down from the ledge, and, close by, what appears
to be a niche hidden in the sheer "walls". NILS risks all and
with a wing and a prayer drops over the edge, feet first, arms
at full stretch reaching out for the bush moments before his
pursuers gallop into view a hundred metres away. With great
strength and gymnastic skill he grabs the plant as he drops,
hangs for a moment then swings in a "half giant swing" and
struggles into a handy square metre-sized semi-concealed
recess in the cliff.

He peers out at the Tigris River, snaking across the valley
floor impossibly far below as the bandits arrive and rein in
their horses. A burly robed bandit approaches the cliff.

> ### BANDIT (ARABIC - LOOKING OVER)
> Unless he had wings, he has gone to the
> black place where all Infidels go. ALLAH
> AKBAR!

He remounts his horse and the demon band gallop away.

#28 INT.CAVE MESOPOTAMIA 1847 FLASHBACKS.DAY/
NIGHT

CLOSE NILS (ALEX) is hunched in the tiny cave and he pulls
out his diary and pencil and a worn and crinkled miniature of a
family posing in a 19th century drawing room next to an antique
piano. The FATHER's grey bearded and stern, the white haired
MOTHER fey looking, sitting swaddled on a chair. Beside her,
young NILS clutches a violin. A cherubic little girl looks up ador-
ingly at her brother.

> ### NILS (ALOUD)
> Wonderful little AGNETHA, Mama, Papa.
> God bless you my beloved family....

He falls asleep and dreams as the picture shrivels and wrinkles to
the mounting crackle of fire

#29 FLASHBACK SOUND AND IMAGE DISSOLVE TO:

INT.danish country house 1819 - NIGHT. FIRST FLASHBACK
IN SERIES. DANISH & english sub titles
NILS is 1O again. The portrait session stops when his father answers a loud banging on the front door

NILS

Who'd be calling so late PAPA?

MOVING - NILS runs after him up the corridor and watches in
horror as his father opens the door to the same threatening brute
who frightened him in the garden at the story's beginning.

MAN

You'll pay me that 'money or the whole
village will know you as SALSTROM the
adulterer for the rest of your life. Now
where's your decrepit shrew of a wife?

NILS stands next to his father trembling.

LARS SALSTROM

She's dying, you scoundrel. I'll pay you
nothing! Ever!

Scurry back to your rat hole or you'll spend
five long years in the Copenhagen dungeons.
I'm off to the authorities at night's end.

The man strikes LARS and he falls heavily. NILS cowers but the
brute shoves the terrified boy to the floor as well before running
off. SOUND DISSOLVE

#30 INT.SALSTROM HOME NIGHT 1819

SOUND DISSOLVE TO deafening fire crackling and roaring.
Distressed voices are shouting, screaming. Young NILS stands at
the end of his bed in the illuminated dark. Flames lick at his bed,
walls, rafters and floor. He hears his sister scream but is welded to
the spot. When the window suddenly shatters he steps onto the
ledge. It's four metres down to the garden. Neighbours are running frantically with buckets of water, shouting instructions. A
chubby maternal woman's pacing below.

HEDWIG

NILS! Jump darling. Do not look back. I can
catch you. Jump...

ON NILS. He's devastated by his sister and mother's cries but cannot save them. He seems to suddenly fall into some kind of trance
and topples off the ledge into HEDWIG's arms. She hugs him and
they watch in horror as the house surrenders to the inferno.
Traumatized, NILS suddenly spies the man who hit his father on
the fringe of the crowd, watching in delight. The boy's now fear-
less and runs at the man, a spirit possessed, and starts punching
him as male neighbours intervene.

YOUNG NILS

This man struck father. He has lit this fire
and killed them all!

The BRUTE hurls NILS, shoves two approaching men to the ground and disappears into the darkness. CUT TO

#31 INT.COPENHAGEN ORPHANAGE.NIGHT.FLASHBACK 1819

MOVING: Ten year old NILS is being led into a grim and Gothic looking Copenhagen orphanage by a living cadaver: the WARDEN (grim, evil faced, balding, in undertaker style suit with long tails). NILS looks back in despair on the gas-lit part of the Old city before entering the dimly lit labyrinth.

NILS (FIGHTING TEARS)

Why am I here? You can't. I have a family!
Had..our home..

He sobs when the man "monsters" him along. They pass an wardrobe with a half open door.. NILS notices the shard of a broken 10 centimetre-long wooden cross.

WARDEN

Those days are behind you now whelp.
Forget all you ever knew, for here I am a God
that listens not to the prayers of children.

Whispering, distressed and sobbing children's voices pervade the dark.

GIRL 1

Mama. Where are you Mama? Don't leave
me in this horrible place Mama(sobs)

GIRL 2.

I promise to be good. Please uncle.

GIRL 2

I'm frightened ...when will you come for me
aunty? Uncle MIKKEL?

41

Voices are soon subsumed by snores and sniffles. Nils sits bolt upright in his bed bent on escape and regards lines of beds that stretch the length of the sinister room. He hears a faint noise and watches in disbelief as the Warden approaches the nearby bed of a little girl of about 4. The WARDEN holds a tallow candle.

WARDEN (WHISPERS)
Come with me child.

The cadaverous Warden leads the sleepy child towards the hallway, the candle flickering. NILS follows silently. He grabs the long sharp shard of cross from the wardrobe and follows them into a foul ablutions block. The warden stands before the sleepy innocent, evil in his eyes. But as he touches the Girl's hair NILS is a diminutive sprinting missile with a wooden broken cross shaft he drives into the Warden's leg, embedding it deeply and steals the door key. The warden's screams are enough to wake the dead, but by the time the torches are lit, NILS is hurrying down Copenhagen's dark streets with the fatigued toddler clinging to his neck.

#32 EXT HEDWIG'S HOUSE COPENHAGEN.DAYBREAK.
FLASHBACK

NILS lays the tiny sleeping girl on his neighbour HEDWIG's doorstep. He places a note in her hand, pounds on the door and runs off to hide as the door is opened a minute later.

HEDWIG
Poor little Poppet. Well I never shall
abandon you little darling. And what's this
note?

(She lovingly picks up the child and peers into darkness).
Is it you young NILS? Are you out there
alone in the dark NILS? My SVEN has
relented. You can live with us. You cannot
survive out there alone Darling. NILS! Please
come inside.

NILS watches tearfully as Hedwig takes the child inside the warmly lit house and the door closes. FADE TO BLACK DISSOLVE TO - Flash forward

#33 SUPER: COPENHAGEN 1825, SIX YEARS LATER

EXT. COPENHAGEN STREET 1825 - NIGHT. 3RD FLASH-BACK

NILS, now a strong semi-feral youth of 16, stands in darkness peering longingly through a curtain slit covering the window of a homely cottage. From his POV a couple and their five children cheerfully eat a late supper. He walks up the dark street past an Ale House and glances in as he passes and recoils in shock when he sights his family's destroyer drunkenly arguing with the inn keeper. Across the street NILS watches the door open and "TRI-CORN" lurch out the door and debauch up the dark street. NILS follows close - ducking in and out of the shadows. Tricorn pauses and urinates a torrent into a stairwell. Nils suddenly emerges from the shadows.

> NILS
>
> Do you remember me Tricorn? Five years
> have passed...

> MAN
>
> Who goes there? Be off with you young
> vagabond before I give you a thrashing.
> Where in Hell d'you come from anyway,
> boy?

The man steps towards NILS trying to discern his face.

> NILS
>
> Aye, Hell's my home. Now breathe your last
> you Dog!

As with the WARDEN, NILS sprints at him like a battering ram, but he's a very powerful street-hardened young man now, and drives his dagger into the thug's stomach up to the hilt. The man topples down the steps and breaks his neck. NILS' shining eyes are the only light in the night.

#34 INT.CLIFF CAVE.ZAGROS MOUNTAINS 1847 MORNING

Back in his cave NILS wakes at first light and tries to shake his nightmares. He shudders in the cold, flicks a scorpion off his arm with a knife and peers out of his "eagle's nest cave". He resolves to try to escape the cave.

> ### NILS (WRITING IN DIARY)
> I cannot die here alone in this Godforsaken
> place?

Through sheer strength, skill and some luck, he half kneels on the sturdy horizontal bush that saved him and digs hand divets in the cliff above him with his knife. There's another smaller plant higher up that supports his weight for a few seconds as he hauls himself over the lip of the bluff. He lies on the cliff top looking up at the scudding clouds in exhaustion before making another diary entry.

> ### MORNING FEBRUARY? 1847
> The sun shines on me anew. I am
> miraculously delivered from death's dark
> vale, but wherefore does such a wretch as I
> merit Providence?

TRACKING: Injured, bleeding, and parched with thirst he wanders deliriously for days before stumbling into the mountain forest "glimpsed" by NILS (as ALEX) in Tasmania at the start of the story. Maple, pistachio and ash trees punch through a ground canopy of sub alpine fern and thick low ground plants.
The forest materializes as he surmounts a low tree-filled hill. It's all too familiar. He fires his pistol to scare off a lion drinking from the stream and he's near death when he collapses in this glade, by a unique prehistoric looking fern. He sleeps for a long time and is awoken by rain. He munches some of the plant's leaves and berries, stuffs some in his pocket and eats some nearby mushrooms.

#35 EXT. ZAGROS MOUNTAIN WILDERNESS. 1847 DAY

MOVING - The mushrooms are hallucinogenic and he's soon floundering through a "psychedelic forest", hopelessly lost. He tries to run again but he suddenly seems to fall into another body – that of GILGAMESH - just for a second and as he looks at his hand he's holding a bronze spear. It's unclear whether or not he's totally hallucinating as he staggers and falls with a look of abject terror, hits his head on a tree root protruding from the mossy ground and falls unconscious. DISSOLVE TO NIGHT

#36 EXT. MOUNTAIN WILDERNESS MORNING.1847

When he awakes, he's miraculously impossibly younger, free of wounds and the Tuberculosis, but it's a day later. Shortly after setting off he stumbles on another stream. When he sees his watery reflection he's both shocked and ecstatic as he's younger by about 25 years.

NILS
Oh sweet JESUS! This must be the magical
plant of the legends! My youth's returned,
my agues gone.

He sniffs himself, as the leaves also generate abnormal amounts of pheromones and writes another Diary Entry:
The magical plant has changed my smell..
now like roasted chestnut

He turns, looking for the forest, but it's disappeared into a hazy distance: DISSOLVE TO

#37 EXT. MESOPOTAMIA SOUTH OF BAGHDAD. 1847. DAY.

Days later he's clearly travelled far on foot. Sighting his "army's" distant base sees some mercenary friends, but he's "done" with soldiering and detours round the ancient fort.

NILS(ALOUD)
Farewell forever my comrades. May Fortune favour each and every one of you till the end of your days.

#38 EXT. SOUTH OF BAGHDAD - DAY 1847

The following morning he stumbles on a dead ARAB warrior, being eaten by hyenas. They reluctantly withdraw some metres, growling at him as he approaches. The ARAB's un-tethered horse grazes nearby. NILS hides his uniform under rocks and removes the corpse's clothing. A dismembered hand falls out of the jalaba as he shrugs it on. Astride the Arab horse, in his tribal robes, boots and face-concealing head gear, he "looks the part" galloping along the sands of the Shat El Arab to the distant sea shimmering in the sun. FADE TO BLACK.

#39 EXT/INT. ANTIQUE SHOP PARIS - DUSK. 1848

AARON, an old JEWISH antiquarian is about to close his antique shop for the night when NILS, now looking to be a handsome man of about 30 again, taps him on the shoulder.

> ### NILS
> Bonsoir Monsieur. Grant me ten minutes
> of your time and you won't regret it. I have
> brought you something special.

The cluttered shop is a treasure trove. NILS produces the golden dagger.

> ### ISAAC
> Mon Dieu Monsieur! A masterpiece from
> the ancient world. Babylonian I think. And
> what rubies! How did you come by such a

treasure? Ce ne fait rien, for you are now
a very wealthy man. Return tomorrow at
this hour and I shall have a buyer for this -
another who knows its true worth..at least
five million francs je crois!

NILS walks out into the windy Paris night grinning. DISSOLVE
TO

#40 EXT. SCANDINAVIAN GARDEN DANISH VILLAGE.
DAY 1848

He is crestfallen when he wanders in his once beautiful garden,
now overgrown and untamed.
From his POV: the burned out derelict remains of the once magnificent house. NILS looks down in sadness on his family picture
once as he walks away. Fifty metres away he sees a blonde haired
woman in her mid thirties standing in his neighbour HEDWIG's
garden.
She holds fresh flowers and stares at him. When he walks past
her he doffs his cap and they exchange a strange look. As a wind
springs up he has a sudden memory flash, realizing she was the
child he saved at the orphanage. As he is about to turn the corner
into a lane he turns his head and sees her hurrying after him and
waving. He can't face her though and flees. All other sounds are
now subsumed by the growing cacophony of a schoolyard: DIS-
SOLVE TO:

#41 INT. WICKLOW HISTORY CLASSROOM.2027 PRESENT

Returning to present the end of period siren sounds. ALEX's
students don't wait to be dismissed but bolt as the film continues.
Only one amorous couple is unsure about ALEX's condition and
they peer towards the back of the classroom where he sits. The
projector flickers white light on the screen as it finishes. When
one of their friends calls them they forget him and exit.
As the spool revolves noisily, ALEX (NILS) suddenly falls onto
the floor. He wakes looking up through glazed eyes at the shy
English Head ROWENA. He's disoriented, speaking slowly.

ALEX (DAZED,DANISH AND ENGLISH)

I lost them all forever! Is it really you
ELIZABETH?

ROWENA

No, not ELIZABETH. And I don't speak
Danish either if that's what you were
speaking?

ALEX (COMING INTO FOCUS)

I'm sorry. What am I saying? That's
impossible. But you do look so like a woman
I knew long ago. I only need this job till
Christmas. Could you..

ROWENA

I won't tell anyone..but..

I should drive you to a hospital. I wonder
though if

it's fair on your students and colleagues,
teaching in this condition. I'm ROWENA
JAMES. Head of English

ALEX

Thank you. I mean it. I'm ALEX..

ROWENA
Some of your colleagues half believe you might be an axe murderer. I was about to suggest you should come to the Staff dinner tomorrow night.. ..meet everyone. Maybe tell me about ELIZABETH. Might be smarter for you to visit Outpatients though.

ALEX
No hospitals. Thanks for the invite, but I doubt I'll make it.

#42 EXT/INT. MUSIC ROOM.WICKLOW – DAY

ROWENA is in the corridor but sticky-beaks looking in to ALEX's room: he's wowing the marginalized kids again. He spies her and SIMON, (small, un-confident Science teacher thick glasses), incredulously staring through the window.

ALEX (MOUTHING THE WORD)
Hello.

ROWENA
Hello yourself..

The watching pair are impressed; the students are rapt. Alex looks at the wall clock and ceases as suddenly as he started, lays the Fender on the desk and writes something on the board. Rowena is gob smacked and still watching the class as the period bell rings. She hurries away.

#43 INT.SCHOOL CORRIDOR. DAY

ROWENA
Dream on ROWENA! A man like that and a widow nearing menopause!

ROWENA's class stream out into the corridor.

SIOBHAN
Where have you been Miss? I marked the
roll for you because we thought you'd run
away to join Cirque Du Soleil.

TRACY
No not the circus - she means the NAVY
Mrs JAMES.

#44 INT. ROOM. WICKLOW - SAME END OF SCHOOL DAY

ALEX has these kids for Home Group too. They sit and stare.

ALEX
I'm Mister SELKIRK! I know it's late in the
day for introductions but TIME is relative as
you too shall discover soon enough.

Some think he's crazy. He now stuns them and rattles off all their
names. No one notices the door open.

ALEX
So, um, before you head off for a weekend
playing Grand Theft Auto or base Jumping,
or whatever it is you do, know this: I am not
the Antichrist. If any of You have problems
and you need help you only need ask. If I
can't fix it I'll find someone who can. BUT!
Remember my one Commandment. No
more bullying. Not physical, verbal, texting
or email. No more of that shite in this place.
Ever! And one last message..!

He sings the uplifting 60's pop song "Try a Little Kindness" as
well as Glen Campbell's version. They're silent but positive when
he finishes the encouraging song.

ALEX

Enough already! Have a good weekend.

The disgruntled headmaster stands in the doorway as they noisily file out.

#45 INT. WICKLOW MUSIC ROOM. DAY

CARL FROBISHER (AWKWARDLY)

I couldn't help hearing your last little polemic
about bullying SELKIRK - care to elaborate?

ALEX (PACKING UP HIS THINGS)

Well, I think bullying here is endemic and
ruining far too many young lives!

CARL

You've been here one day! Listen, we already
have an approved protection policy and it's..

ALEX

Not BLOODY working! Sorry but there's at
least Four kids in this class alone whose lives
are a misery from it. And I wonder if you've
seen the guys

ALEX CONT

in skull masks around this place. That can't
be healthy.

CARL's seen them. He's apparently never been challenged like this
and has no rejoinder. After an awkward silence he walks away
exasperated.

#46 EXT. ROAD OUTSIDE WICKLOW SCHOOL. AFTER-
NOON

Students line up outside a row of buses. Impatient parents in cars add to the congestion. Its chaos when the rain starts again. Alex is on bus duty sheltering under an umbrella. He tries to keep some order but suddenly spies his student DAMIEN and his sister GRETEL hurrying up the street while a dark car with tinted windows drives slowly alongside them. Alex can see a man's arm gesturing violently at them and even though they are at a distance, they're obviously fearful and trying to escape him. NILS drops his brolly and races up the street towards them and quickly closes on the car. The window's not fully down but Alex gets a momentary look at the heavy-set man with the week-long stubble.

ALEX (DIALING ON MOBILE)
Hey! What the hell're you doing bothering these kids? I'm calling the police and giving them your licence plate number..

HARLEY GREENWOOD (YELLS)
Fuck off Chalkie.

GREENWOOD doesn't turn to face ALEX, but flattens the accelerator and roars off. Alex watches as he jerks his raised arm out the window and gives him the extended finger. Damien and Gretel are both totally distressed and drenched as Alex approaches them.

ALEX
Did that man threaten you..?

GRETEL (HUMILIATED)
Please Mr SELKIRK don't call the police.. he's our..father.

ALEX, nods awkwardly as the kids squirm.

ALEX (HANDING OVER HIS UMBRELLA)
Take my car keys. It's the dark blue Peugeot. Stay dry. I'll be drive you home in about ten.

#47 EXT.WICKLOW SCHOOL ENTRANCE.DAY

ALEX is saturated. He trudges to the front entrance doors where ROWENA stands, having observed all of the drama.

> ROWENA
> So you've met the lovely Mr HARLEY GREENWOOD?

> ALEX:
> Those poor kids! The local psycho dad: An unemployable thug.

> ROWENA
> Try "defrocked" Pharmacist.

(ALEX is amazed)
> Struck off for illegal drug manufacture. Barring a miracle, he's heading for Risdon Gaol unless he rats on his bosses and dealers. Very scary guy, Mr GREENWOOD. He's an ex boxer as well.

#48 INT.COFFEE SHOP.HOBART MALL.MORNING

On a Saturday morning ALEX sits alone in a coffee shop reading the paper about HARLEY. A close view of the article suggests he might have had accomplices in high places as most of the evidence has disappeared from police secure storage.

#49 EXT. DERWENT RIVER WALK – MORNING

On the same weekend morning Sally, Gretel and Damien stroll along a river bank to a shopping centre.

> SALLY
> ...durr! Of course he's a great muso but definitely from La La Land though. He seems a bit crazy.

DAMIEN

NNot crazy, mm more like a sol- itary. It's k kind of obvious.

SALLY

To you maybe! 'Cause it takes one to know one right!

GRETEL

I bet he could teach us to sing, as well as play guitars?

DAMIEN

H.hhe might. WWow! He sure can ppplay though. Mmakes you wonder why ...

GRETEL

Yeah! Why a crummy school like Wicklow? When he could play in a Rock band or Jazz Band in...

SALLY

Anywhere!

GRETEL (NODDING)

And teacher or no teacher, he sure kept THEM in line. No one's ever done that before. Even those awful boys Chad and Wayne seemed scared of him

DAMIEN

I've ggot a bbbad feeling about them. Maybe not MMMARTY but. .

GRETEL
That won't happen now. You heard Sir..

Then almost 'on cue', they pass a lane-way by the river path and these boys emerge from the lane.

CHAD
Well look who it is! HO 1, HO 2 AND HO-MO. Who told you Homies you could use this pathway?

He and WAYNE laugh and give each other high fives. They look as though they're going to hurt DAMIEN but MARTY diverts them. He occasionally glances at SALLY.

MARTY (WITHOUT CONVICTION)
Ahr what're we doin' here! Let's fuck off to the Mall. Im cold AS. Let's ditch these losers.

They all wander off up the lane again, CHAD sprays graffiti along the fence as they go. SALLY glances after MARTY.

#50 INT.THE REPUBLIC PUB. HOBART.SATURDAY NIGHT

ALEX scans the Republic - an Aussie time capsule of a pub, with a fascinating cross section of humanity ranging from the early 1930's to Hippies to Punks, Goths to "mid 22nd century". ALEX and the Polynesian BOUNCERS, recognize each other as men of action. JESS waves to ALEX and leads him to a back room where about twenty teachers and their partners sit at a long trestle table. He sits at the end next to Rowena. He looks uncomfortable and most of them appear somewhat merry. CLOSE ON ROWENA She has lovely face and figure, but makes no effort no effort with her appearance. HILARY (25, petite trendy Fashionista brunette, heavy make- up) and Sports master JASON, (muscular, blond jock), are sitting opposite. HILARY and JESS confer about ALEX. JASON strains to listen. He's drunk too many beers already and is the jealous type with clear personal issues. ROWENA glances often at ALEX

JESS
Hi ALEX. Glad you could make it. Come
and meet everybody. CARL, you've met, and
this is COLLETTE, RANALD and...

The threesome don't look too welcoming. She guides him to a
spare seat near her friends.

JESS(MISCHIEVIOUS: A BIT TIPSY)
And finally my gal pal fashion diva
HILARY..and JASON, my lamb with the
golden fleece. (Ruffles his blond locks) I
mean ram!

JASON
Not funny JENNIFER!

JESS
Sorry. JASON'S divorce came though
yesterday.

JASON's armour's pierced. JENN's flirty and tactile with ALEX and JASON doesn't like it one bit.

JESS
AND this Lady sitting here is my frien...

HILARY
Her great, great, great aunt ROWENA. An old, old friend.

ROWENA's embarrassed and hurt by the bitchy jibe.

ROWENA
ALEX and I have met. HIL thinks she's bullet proof. Remember what the Pygmies say though HIL: "Life is short"!

There's awkward silence. SIMON (timid, social-phobic, diminutive,) joins her gripping a sheet of paper, seemingly intent on talking to ALEX.

ROWENA
Hi SIMON. How did your mum's scan go?

SIMON (EMBARRASSED RED FACED)
No change. Chemo's just awful! Erm, we haven't met, ALEX, but I wondered erm...

ALEX (HE'S BEEN LIKE THIS ONCE)
Hello. You're Maths and Science, right?

(SIMON nods and produces a page of typed writing).
And I'm guessing you've written a song!
Good on you! Sure, I can have a go at setting it to music.

SIMON
Maybe more like a poem. I called it "THE PERFECT MARIGOLD"

SIMON
Erm, I have visit the hospital, so...very kind of you. Bye ROWENA..... ALEX..

He ambles out hunch-shouldered. HILARY watches him go and half whispers to JESS, but it's audible to ALEX

HILARY
What a Loser! Why do so many "small men" become teachers?

HILARY
Must be the last refuge of the Moribund male!

ALEX

I thought Losers were people who give up.
Guaranteed this'll be better than most could
write. As for Small men and Little Women,
we're everyone one of us mostly one or the
other.

HILARY glares at him, an enemy for life. ROWENA's impressed.
JESS's drunk and flirts with ALEX.

JASON (DRUNK, JEALOUS)

So, ALEX, a Musician! Where are yer from
then? Europe or somewhere?

ALEX

Somewhere! Yes. Pretty much.

JASON

You play any football over there? No! I
reckon you're not the type for contact
Sports... You'd be too .. MUSICAL!

ALEX(W.C FIELDS COMIC VOICE)

Ah ye-e- es! FOOTBAWLLL! The true
measure of a maaan!

JASON (BITING)

I didn't mean MUSICAL I was going to say
OLD actually.

ALEX (LAUGHS LOUDLY)

You have no idea!

JASON's peeved and all except ROWENA thinks he's an oddball.

JASON

So - How many languages DO you speak
SALSTORM?

He mispronounces the name intentionally.

ALEX(WRY, MISCHIEVOUS)
Pretty much ALL of them I think!

They don't know what to make of him and it irks them. Teachers
have a need to pigeon hole. ROWENA smirks.

RANALD (OLD SCHOOL ACADEMIC TYPE)
I just twigged to your name. ALEX-ANDER
SELKIRK was DANIEL DEFOE's real life
castaway model for ROBINSON CRUSOE.

A few colleagues regard ALEX suspiciously.

ALEX (WHISPERING TO ROWENA)
Yeah it's not who-you-know but
HUGUENOT.(THEN ALOUD): My parents
were literary types, and SELKIRK, the real
CRUSOE, was an ancestor.

JASON
Hey VITA, can you come over here for a
minute? I need you to talk some TONGAN
with this bloke.

The giant Polynesian Bouncer is busy, and crankily gestures for
JASON to stop drinking. ALEX is suddenly grey-faced ill and
excuses himself. ROWENA watches him in concern.
Ext.public bar area republic pub.night
Passing a corner of the large bar area ALEX notices a well-dressed
hard man who looks slightly familiar. It's HARLEY GREEN-
WOOD and he's approaching two other sizable men who look
like off duty cops. Harley's drunk. The other 2 wander into another bar to avoid him.

#51 EXT.REPUBLIC BAR CARPARK.NIGHT.

ALEX stumbles out into the packed dark car park. A half-moon and the pub veranda light provide the only illumination. He throws up and staggers along a row of cars and half lies against the bonnet of a big four- wheel drive thirty metres from the entrance. He suddenly slides off the car down to the asphalt and lies down, breathing almost asthmatically. He's shuddering slightly when he hears two people coming down the steps and walking close by and a third follows them out. Under the car body he sees a pair of feet approach the other two pairs of feet in a confrontational way.

> DETECTIVE JACK SNOWDEN
> You know better than to come here
> HARLEY. I've told you –

> DETECTIVE SNOWDON
> Never approach me or BILL in a public place
> again. I'll contact YOU when I need to see
> you. Capiche?

He now takes an envelope from his suit coat pocket and hands it to HARLEY.

> HARLEY
> What the fuck is this..?

> SNOWDEN
> Consider it a gift. A first class ticket on the
> five star ferry and two weeks at the six star
> WESTIN in Melbourne. Plus some travelling
> dough. Two weeks out of the spotlight'll do
> you good. And us as well.

> HARLEY
> Very generous of you Turd-face I'll think
> about it.

SNOWDEN (MEASURED, COLD)
Well don't think too long will yer? And when
you get back..if the Police Integrity watch
dogs or Media come callin' make like yer
know nothing about anything or anyone. Do
that and the worst you'll do

is some short easy time in RISDON prison.
Ignore this advice at yer peril. We're going back
inside for a drink. GOOD NIGHT HARLEY!

These two head back to the pub. HARLEY's drunk.

HARLEY GREENWOOD
Fuck you yer limp dick Flatfoot. I go where I
want and if you bastards don't help me beat
this you'll all go down with me.

ALEX sees the men freeze at the top of the stairs, turn their heads
towards HARLEY for a second and disappear inside. HARLEY
urinates against a car before following them back in. ALEX
struggles to his feet and pulls a medicine vial from his pocket and
swigs from it.

#52 INT. REPUBLIC BAR HOBART. AFTER MIDNIGHT

FROM bouncer VITA's surprised POV ALEX looks deathly ill as
he walks gingerly inside towards the bar. He doesn't recognize
Detective SNOWDEN and his mate from the car park lounging
near the bar but sees them watching HARLEY swigging down a
pint of beer from across the room, and visually twigs to who is
who. ALEX buys a soft drink and is heading back towards the
ante room when HARLEY recognizes him and strides towards
him bent on a fight. ALEX turns instinctively just as VITA steps
between them.

HARLEY GREENWOOD
We're not done yet Chalkie. Not by a fucking
long shot!

VITA nods at the exit. ALEX and HARLEY's eyes meet threat-eningly before Harley exits. SNOWDEN and friend watch the incident with interest.

#53 INT.REPUBLIC BAR ANTE ROOM.

ROWENA studies ALEX as JEN flirts with him again. JASON pushes a chair between them and sits. ROWENA gives ALEX a "watch-out" look.

JASON

I reckon you're a wanker SELKIRK. Why
don't you prove me wrong?

Everyone's aghast at his aggression.

ALEX (STILL SICKLY)

What did you have in mind, a pie-eating
contest? And I'd prefer you don't call me by
that name.

66

JASON
Or what? No: an arm wrestle, smart arse! A
test of strength.

ALEX is vaguely amused. No one else is.

JESS
But not strength of character! I'm calling
a taxi. Coming HIL? You're an ugly drunk
JASON. Get your act together or you and I
are history.

She storms out with HILARY trailing in her wake.

JASON (OBLIVIOUS)
Let's do this- if you won't, you're a pissant.

Despite sickness ALEX looks sorry for JASON and surprises all
by easily matching him, but pretends it's a draw and heads for
the toilet. After another violent coughing fit he returns, and finds
JASON's a disaster.

ALEX
Let's go Mate. We'll share a taxi and I'LL get
you Home

JASON (SLURRING)
I'll never be your mate.

ROWENA
No! we'll take my car. I've only had two
glasses of Riesling.

#54 EXT. PUB. NIGHT

JASON's so drunk they almost carry him to her car

> ### JASON (SLURRED SPEECH)
> It's good of you ROWIE But YOU better
> watch out SLEKIRK. I'm onto you. My
> wife....said...she's

ALEX looks at him piteously in the rear-view mirror.
> She's got.. the twins. I lost everything that
> mattered!

#55 INT. GRETEL AND DAMIEN'S HOME - THE SAME
NIGHT.

Inside the GREENWOODS' impoverished Housing Commission Unit, there's at least a homely pride evident and in the pokey lounge-room there's a warmth. DAMIEN and GRETEL sit on the lounge strumming guitars watching Australian Idol, their love of music obvious. Their mother KAREN knits and smiles at her son looking so happy.

> ### DAMIEN
> ..yyeah 'mum, Music's like hhis religion..

GRETEL smiles in agreement. He's more confident.

> ### KAREN GREENWOOD
> He sounds like a nice man DAMIEN. Do
> you realize your stutter's almost gone..

> ### DAMIEN (REMEMBERING)
> ..and he tttold off DAD the other day too..

KATEN'S face blanches.

> ### KAREN GREENWOOD (LONG
> PAUSE)
> What! Your Father.. approached you both?
> At school? Despite the AVO!

#56 INT. ROWENA'S CAR - NIGHT.

JASON's fighting tears.

ROWENA (COMPASSIONATE)
You have to smell the coffee JASON. Focus
on the good things- your two terrific kids,
and you still have a chance with JENN, if..
you'd just stop!

JASON
Stop what?

ALEX
What do you bloody think?

JASON
ROWIE, leave this Dropkick at a taxi stand
and take me to my home will you? Do that
for me now and I'll never ask anything else
of you. Ever! And you go to Hell SELKUNT.

(As ALEX mouths "no" at her)

ROWENA
I detest that word JASON.

As they're driving ALEX instinctively looks over his shoulder as
for a second he suspects a dark car fifty metres back might be
following them. When he checks again moments later, it's gone.
DISSOLVE TO:

#57 EXT.JASON'S FAMILY HOME.NIGHT

ROWENA parks across the road from the cheerfully lit house.
JASON stares blankly and they can briefly see his 12 year old son
and daughter wrestling in the lounge room. CLOSE: Suddenly a
Porsche pulls up outside the house and a well-dressed man of his

age bounds out and up the steps to the front door. ALEX sees JASON's losing it when his estranged wife opens the door and kisses the man and leads him inside. MOVING JASON hurls open the car door and runs across the street towards the house but ALEX tackles him on the lawn near the front steps. ALEX frog marches him back to the car, and eases him into the back seat.

ALEX
Never ever let your family see you like this.
Get off the grog for good and get strong
again and your kids will keep loving you. It's
half past midnight in your life JASON - time
and tide wait for no one, so grow your balls
back and get up off the fucking canvas.

JASON stares at him and vomits on the seat. They wipe him down with a towel, drive him home and leave him on a divan. ROWE-NA'S lays a blanket over him. ALEX writes the AA number on a pad on his bedside table.

#58 INT. ROWENA'S CAR – NIGHT

ROWENA drives along a narrow private road bordered by a high red brick wall on each side till she parks in the roundabout near the driveway to the luxury harbour-side unit complex where he lives.

> ROWENA
> That was harsh! Awful, really: What you said
> to him.

> ALEX
> I've learned through life that addicts need
> tough love!

> ROWENA
> Tough, maybe. Brutal, no!

> ALEX
> Think I'll head inside. Thanks for the lift.

> ROWENA
> Wait.. Can't we just talk?

(She touches his hand. There's real chemistry).
> I don't mean to sound judgmental. I know
> you meant well

> ROWENA

> And I meant what I said at the pub, about
> life being short. I think we both know that..

> ALEX (ENIGMATIC ASIDE)
> Not that short, though: Timor mortis
> conturbat me!

She gives him a quizzical look.

ROWENA
What's that? Time and Death they confound
me? You've read WILLIAM DUNBAR?
Okay, um, here goes nothing: I've been a
widow for six years now. Maybe I'm wrong
but I sense an attraction between us..

ALEX
ROWENA, I'm not who you thi..

ROWENA (SILENCING HIM)
I'm not prepared to die wondering. Just tell
me if you feel something too.

He nods fatalistically. Her fingers caress his hand.
To be honest, I'm fussy and lonely by choice
and I think you are too. I choose not to be
anymore though if you'll give me a chance..

ALEX
You're funny; and strange! But in a good
way. So, sure, I'm attracted to you, but we've
only just met. You don't know me.

ROWENA
You might be surprised. I know you're smart,
caring, and kind. And you probably beat
yourself up a lot.

ALEX
Someone has to.

ROWENA
And you're a worrier. I'd bet my mortgage
you're running from something in your past
too. But the worst thing I

ROWENA CONT

think is that you're possibly dangerously
sick. How am I doing so far?

ALEX

This is scary. Have you read my
autobiography?

ROWENA

No, who wrote it?

ALEX

No friend of mine.

ROWENA (WRY SMILE)

So what's its title?

ALEX

Either "Without a Clue" or "The Vale of
Sorrows". Take your pick.

ROWENA

You're a Smart ALEX aren't you? And a sad
one. Can I just ask one last question? Who
was ELIZABETH? Your wife?

(Long silence).

ALEX

I never married. But I believe I loved her..
War intervened.

ROWENA

You're a Vietnam Veteran? Was she
Vietnamese?

ALEX (IRONIC, SILLY)
Not that I noticed. No, not as such.

He can't help throwaway lines; can't hide his pain. She gives him a puzzled look and changes the subject.

ROWENA
It's tough being alone most of the time isn't it? You seem to have hope though, and that's a good thing.

ALEX
Really? What are your hopes?

ROWENA
I know what matters in life. What I've had and what I've lost. My biggest hope is that one day my only daughter Mary Anne ..she's living in America with a nasty pastie husband...might one day reconcile with me. For a little while I used to hope to possibly meet another..

Their faces are close. She touches his cheek with her hand.
Would you like to come to my house for a home-cooked meal?

He's disarmed as she's just lovely. They kiss once and he gets out and watches her turn and drive away.

#59 EXT.APARTMENT COMPLEX ROAD. NIGHT

He suddenly notices the same dark car he saw earlier, parked in the darkness 100 metres up the street, its motor running. He starts walking up the road towards it. Suddenly the engine revs and it speeds towards him and he has to leap to the top of the wall and swing his legs up high as it narrowly misses him.
He swings his leg up to the top of the wall as the car brakes at the roundabout. Tyres screeching, the car does a wheelie and speeds

back up the road once more towards him and passes underneath him. He waits until it disappears up the road and into a main thoroughfare and some night traffic before dropping to the road and running back towards the gated complex.

#60 EXT. ROOM WICKLOW – DAY

MLS of ALEX through classroom windows from SALLY, DAMIEN and GRETEL's POV. They're summoning up courage to go and see him while he's marking papers.

#61 INT. MUSIC ROOM AFTER SCHOOL

ALEX's sees the kids through the small window in the door.

> ALEX
> Young humid beans! And in a school! What
> a shock!

> GRETEL
> Um, seeing we're in your music class Mr
> SELKIRK..

The kids are great. He's happy for the first time in ages.
> DAMIEN was wondering (DAMIEN
> scowls) um, we ALL were wondering if
> you might teach us to sing as well as play
> better. DAMIEN doesn't own a violin and
> he's really good And SALLY and I just have
> one crummy old guitar between us. This is
> embarrassing

He nods and smiles a definite "yes". They beam

#62 INT. NON VERBAL WICKLOW MONTAGE WITH MUSIC.

ALEX's paternal mentoring gives him a positivism he has never experienced. Dissolves show more kids joining these sessions every day and the bullies getting angrier and feeling more isolated.

#63 INT.MUSIC ROOM – DAY

GRETEL, JOANNA, DAMIEN and SALLY each hold new guitars as ALEX/NILS talks to them. Marty passes by the door way several times feigning disinterest, so Nils calls him in.

> ALEX
> Hey MARTY stop loitering with discontent.
> Get your sorry carcass in here. Now
> remember, singing is almost as important as
> breathing and makes you happy by getting
> endorphins going.

JOANNA
Coldplay's and U2's songs maybe, but what
the heck are endorphins?

ALEX
Ask your science teacher. Listen to some
LEONARD COHEN and NEIL YOUNG, as
they're old school, but great lyricists.

JOANNA
Sounds like funeral music. You should try
stand-up comedy Sir.

#64 INT. ROOM MONTAGE – DAY

MONTAGE: The shy and under-confident kids grow more confident and gradually start to blossom.

FROM THE POV of other teachers, more and more kids start to hang around him when he does his yard duties. Gretel and Sally show particular abilities as singers and are growing into confident young women. Raelene is seen alone watching the music room from a distance. She looks to have a need to change.

#65 INT. COMMON ROOM. DAY 2027

BRONWYN, a teacher's aide (OLDER, GREY, IN A HAND MADE SHAWL), ROWENA, JASON and RANALD are talking over lunch. At another table two teachers are playing chess while a third reads a local newspaper. JESS walks in breezily with a hot dog from the canteen, interrupting their newspaper quiz.

> JESS
> Has anyone looked in on the music room
> lately? ALEX's transforming some of those
> shy kids.

JESS's almost on speaking terms again with JASON

JASON
He's a self-promoting arrogant poser. Time'll prove me right.

JESS
When are you going to grow up and look for the best in people instead of the worst? He's even got that Jock MARTY playing guitar with them!

They're stunned at this.

MEREDITH
I think ALEX is a spunk. He maybe looks like one of GEORGE CLOONEY's elder brothers.

JASON
Yeah! The adopted one! From Tierra del Fuego!

They watch him walk out sullenly.

RANALD
Seriously? MARTY? Now THAT I have to see!

He gets up and four others follow him out.

#66 EXT. MUSIC ROOM – DAY

RANALD and colleagues peer into the music room and marvel at the hive of creativity. MARTY's strumming away RANALD smiles to himself when he notices the youth watching SALLY. They are all impressed. RANALD can only shake his head in disbelief when he sees RAELENE taking an instrument from ALEX.

79

#67 INT. ROOM – DAY

All kids are bonding with ALEX, now a father or elder brother figure as much as a mentor. For once he looks happy. GRETEL's on guitar and DAMIEN's on violin.

ALEX (TO GRETEL ON GUITAR)
Follow me DAMIEN adlib harmony

DAMIEN
Sir? Is there sheet m music for that ELO song the Livin' Thing"?

He's a new person. Even his stutter's disappearing
How about you guys and I play together at
end of term concert?

GRETEL
You really mean it Sir? Could we be good
enough by then? Or are you just joking?

ALEX
I never joke about music.

His obvious satisfaction makes them beam.

#68 MONTAGE – 2027 DAY

A montage shows musicians group growing till it's every day of the week. The originals are getting better and more confident. Some kids passing by are envious. Wayne and Chad are furious with MARTY's "betrayal" and shun him. Principal CARL passes and smiles grudgingly.

#69 EXT. MOUNTAIN FOREST DAY

ALEX is alone in the forest searching for the plant. His despera-tion's growing and health deteriorating
SEVERAL DISSOLVES TO:

He emerges from a copse of ferns and sits in the long grass studying botanical paintings - one a copy of a beautiful JOHN GLOVER painting of flowers and forest.He suddenly gasps as a full grown female Tasmanian Tiger and her cub stop in their tracks a few metres from him. He readies the SLR to take a multi-million dollar photograph, but comes to his senses and he just stares in wonderment.

ALEX(THROWS THEM SOME BEEF JERKY)

Whoa! They said your kind's been extinct
since 1937 but you're still here..and both
magnificent!

The "tigers" aren't frightened. They sniff the meat and gobble it. ALEX takes a step towards them with an outstretched hand. The female makes a rasping sound, and bounds away followed by the pup. ALEX grins as the bush swallows them up.

ALEX
Magical, magical, magical. How bloody
wonderful!

When ALEX emerges from the forest and heads towards his car
in a leafy picnic area, it's dusk. CUT TO:

#70 EXT. DEVONPORT. DUSK. SAME DAY

A line of cars snakes along the harbour drive towards the ship
and brightly lit car ferry Empress of Tasmania.

#71 INT. HARLEY GREENWOOD'S CAR.

He's sniffing cocaine and dressed for a trip. There's an expensive
suitcase on his backseat. He hands a ticket to a uniformed guard
directing the cars onto the ship. DISSOLVE

#72 INT.EXT.HARLEY'S CABIN EMPRESS OF TASMANIA.
NIGHT

He's pleased when he looks in the mirror and heads out for what he clearly hopes for a wild night on the ship.

#73 INT.EMPRESS OF TASMANIA. RESTAURANT/DINING
AREA.

MOVING. HARLEY looks confident but aggressive as he strides
past the dining area checking out every woman he sees, partnered or
not. He pauses at a door to the deck, opens it slightly to a cold wind
and glances back at the receding dock-land lights as the ship sails
out into the darkness. He slams the door shut and heads along the
corridor again. At the entrance to the crowded bar he checks out the
scene before heading for a vacant bar stool near three attractive and
fairly provocatively dressed mid-forties women in alcohol lubricated
conversation. He appraises them and leers at the blondest of them
and sits on the tall stool and orders drinks.

HARLEY GREENWOOD

Get me a double shot of Tequila and a
Corona thanks mate. And a round on me of
whatever these gorgeous ladies are having.

They're already half tipsy and easily impressed. The blonde raises her
champagne glass to him in thanks.
DISSOLVE TO: Two hours later he's struck out with the women
and they're no longer impressed with him as they exit. He's happily
boozy though and staring out through the thick window at a storm
whipping the white plumes on black waves when a heavily made up
younger woman in a black wig and low cut little black dress comes
and sits next to him. Any sober person would tread warily as she
looks like a high end prostitute and seems to have an agenda, as she
immediately engages HARLEY in conversation, touching his hand as
they talk.
Through the crowd of voluble drinkers two partly obscured solid
men in casual dress seem to be watching the proceedings. From their
point of view the woman and Harley are very quickly getting frisky.

HARLEY (SWIGGING DOWN
ANOTHER DRINK)

So what'd you say your name was?

83

> ### WOMAN
> I didn't, but it's CHANELLE...

> ### HARLEY GREENWOOD
> Thought I recognized that smell - surname
> Number Five? I s'pose a fuck'd be out of the
> question?

Her sultry grin answers him and they laugh. He pulls out his room key and puts it in her hand and places his own hand on her thigh. They stand uncertainly as the ship pitches in the worsening weather.

> ### WOMAN
> ..but I think I'll go out on deck for a few
> minutes and get some fresh air first...

He looks out at the blackening night and is shocked as she heads for the doors to the deck.

> ### HARLEY (CALLING AFTER HER)
> Yer can't be serious!

He baulks for a second but with a lascivious look he reluctantly walks somewhat uncertainly after her.

#74 EXT.DECK WALKWAY EMPRESS OF TASMANIA.NIGHT.

The deck's dark and deserted outside and the dark roiling waters look threatening. The wind is up and rain starts to fall as he searches the deck for her. He lurches along with the pitching deck and swears just audibly in the wind.

> ### HARLEY GREENWOOD
> CHANELLE? Where'd you go?

Somewhere behind him there's a flash of light as someone opens and closes the bar door. He's unaware and struggles along the walkway against the wind pausing only to lean against the railing and look out to sea. Suddenly three solid FIGURES appear out of the darkness behind him and lift him by the legs and head simultaneously in a fluid moment and he's suddenly flailing over the ballustrade towards the black sea, his cry swallowed by the night storm. MOVING: the three assailants race up the storm lashed deck and disappear back into the ship through a distant door..

#75 INT. WICKLOW HIGH. MORNING

It's recess and Alex is having a coffee and listening to the radio mounting horror. NEWSREADER: LOCAL DISGRACED PHARMACIST AND BANNED DRUG INQUEST SUSPECT HARLEY GREENWOOD IS MISSING PRESUMED DEAD AFTER BOARDING THE EMPRESS OF TASMANIA FOR MELBOURNE LATE YESTERDAY AFTERNOON. GREENWOOD'S BLACK FORD WAS FOUND UNCLAIMED IN THE SHIP'S PARKING HOLD AND AFTER INVESTIGATION HIS CABIN WAS FOUND UNTOUCHED AND HIS BED UN-SLEPT IN. HE WAS SEEN TALKING TO SEVERAL WOMEN DURING A LONG DRINKING SESSION IN THE SHIP'S BAR BUT THE IDENTITY OF ANOTHER MYSTERY WOMAN IN BLACK LAST SEEN TALKING TO HIM HAS NOT BEEN DISCOVERED.

> ROWENA (JOINING HIM WITH A COFFEE)
> What's happened? You're As white as a proverbial..

He shushes her.

> NARRATOR
> INVESTIGATORS BELIEVE SHE WAS DISGUISED AND HAVE NO DOUBT THERE HAS BEEN FOUL PLAY.

> ALEX (SWITCHES DOWN THE SOUND)
> It's that bastard GREENWOOD…he's missing presumed dead yesterday.

> ROWENA
> Sorry if I don't sound sad. But isn't that a Godsend.

> ALEX:
> Hugely, for his family and this city. But he and I had a ..run-in at the pub two weeks ago. There were witnesses and I'll be a suspect. Guaranteed!

> ROWENA
> Well..if anyone asks we're having an affair. Remember carefully now: we spent that weekend together...mostly in bed fornicating, sleeping, drinking my two gift bottles of Mumm champagne, eating lasagna and garlic bread I made us and.. That's all she wrote. Are you okay with that?

He's speechlessly grateful. DISSOLVE TO:

#76 INT.WICKLOW.DAY

At the end of the day ALEX's students are exiting as a younger student appears at the door and hands him a note.

#77 INT.HEADMASTER'S OFFICE.DAY

He knocks and enters. Two uniformed cops are there and Detective SNOWDEN. NILS realizes what's happened but Snowden's oblivious to ALEX's knowledge.

> HEADMASTER CARL
> I'm sorry to have summoned you without warning ALEX but Detective Snowden here has some..

SNOWDEN
Witnesses have identified you as being
involved in an altercation at the Republic
pub on Saturday night the 7th of this month
with one, HARLEY DALE GREENWOOD,
currently missing presumed dead.

(ALEX looks suitably stunned). Where were
you Sunday the 8th SELKIRK?

ALEX
I know who you're talking about but I never
knew the guy till he abused me that Saturday
night. I spent the rest of the weekend till
Monday morning with my lady. Anyone who
says I was involved in his disappearance is a
liar...

Snowden's disappointed but demands proof.

ALEX: (EMBARRASSED)
Sorry CARL.ROWENA and I are in a
relationship.

CARL's amazed and red faced. He makes an internal call. DIS-
SOLVE TO:

#78 EXT/INT HEADMASTER'S OFFICE.DAY

ROWENA knocks and enters looking apprehensive.
From the POV of a student passing the window SNOWDEN is
interrogating Rowena and Alex. He looks exasperated.

ALEX:
One self-defensive altercation with an aggro
drunk and accused criminal doesn't make
me the prime suspect in anything.

SNOWDEN.
That'll be all for now then. We'll be in touch.

Alex looks to be considering how to deal with Snowden. He nods gratefully to Rowena and Carl. DISSOLVE TO

#79 INT. SHOPPING CENTRE – DAY

ROWENA enters a smart clothing boutique. DISSOLVE TO:
She exits with a number of bags and enters a shoe shop likewise.
DISSOLVE TO:

#80 SALON HOBART – DAY

She enters an up-market beauty shop and raises her eyebrows at the stylish "team" as if to say "give me the works".

#81 INT. ROWENA'S HOUSE – NIGHT

From ALEX's POV she's breathtakingly beautiful as she opens the door - transformed into a glamorous siren.

> ### ALEX
> ROWENA! Crikey!

She's laughs at his STEVE IRWIN voice and escorts him in. A series of romantic dissolves: The night goes well. They sit facing each other, the chemistry obvious.

> ### ROWENA
> You really have lived a life less ordinary,
> haven't you?

His reaction shows she's right. He checks out photos on a nearby display cabinet. One is of a woman of about 30 cradling an infant. She looks like Rowena.

> ### ALEX
> Your daughter and grand- daughter? They
> live in U.S.A

> ### ROWENA (SUDDENLY UPSET)
> MARY-ANNE. And LOUISE is three

> ### ALEX
> And you and LOUISE're not just estranged ..
> you've never met the child, yeah? And.. you
> blame her husband?

> ### ROWENA (FIGHTING TEARS)
> He breaks her heart. But your children - you
> can't tell them anything!

ALEX now picks up a photo of a man aged about fifty.

ROWENA
Bone cancer took NEAL six years ago. He
was good dad and husband. I haven't been
with anyone since.

He sits next to her on the lounge. They're close

ROWENA
ALEX....

They kiss passionately while hurriedly removing each other's
clothing.

MONTAGE: They have wonderful wild sex and it's a special night
for both of them. DISSOLVE TO:

#82 INT.ROWENA'S HOUSE.MORNING

In the bathroom the following morning, though he's coughing blood once more and has another fit. ROWENA wakes to a thumping noise and runs to him. He's catatonic again so she places a blanket over him and a pillow under his head and awaits his recovery. He finally starts to come out of it as she strokes his head.

> ### ROWENA
> Would you... think about me staying over with you? Just for a few days a week - on a trial basis of course. You really do need someone to look after you. Be part time partners? You do know we could love each other. Don't you?

> ### ALEX (GETTING UP SMILING)
> You're a suitable case for treatment ROWIE? We've barely met.

#83 INT. COMMON ROOM – DAY

ROWENA's late to a staff meeting and you could hear a pin drop as every face in the room stares at her. She's stunning. The younger females, especially HILARY, are speechless, the likewise, "seeing her" as if for the first time. ALEX smiles to himself: ROWENA the bombshell!

#84 INT. HISTORY AUDIO VISUAL ROOM WICKLOW HIGH.DAY

ALEX is showing a doco about the SOMME Campaign of 1916 to senior students. As he sits at the back and watches he once more enters the catatonic state as it evokes a vivid memory. A girl of about 18 whispers to her friend and they peer back at him in the darkness. He's sitting oddly, propped against the wall.

> ### GIRL 1
> Is that bloke alright JAN? Should we check him?

GIRL 2
Course not! Teachers that age doze off all the
time.

DISSOLVE TO FADE IN SUPER

1914 SUPER: **LONDON, JULY 1914**

THE BLACK AND WHITE FOOTAGE OF 1914 LONDONERS
AND SOLDIERS DISSOLVES INTO A GRAINY SEPIA COLOUR.

#85 LONDON STREETS. AUGUST 2, 1914

TRACKING through the crowd outside the shop. It's raining.
From POV of a grimy street urchin pick-pocket (about 10), ALEX
(STILL KNOWN AS NILS BACK THEN) hurries along a cob-
ble-stoned street carrying an unconscious girl of about 14 in his
arms. He's an athletic 40 again. He enters gloomy St Stephens
Anglican Orphanage. The surprised urchin follows his mark into
the "maze of alleyways, keeping just out of eyeshot. Nils follows
the NUNS to a basic ward and lays the girl on a bed. He over-
whelms them with a large financial gift.

SISTER HARRIETT

Your generosity and kindness honour our
institution Sir.

ALEX

Can't you save her? She's just a child.

SISTER JUDITH (SHAKING HER HEAD)

Her syphilis is advanced and she's also
Tubercular. The lass will be in God's hands
soon enough. I'm sorry, but we get children
like her every day.

The dying girl looks up at him fearfully. She can't even speak. The
sisters leave briefly as he talks to her and gives the girl the "elixir"
leaves mixed in a cup of water.

NILS

Drink this Sweetheart. It will truly help
you. And take this. (He now gives a wad
of pounds in a wallet and a note). When
you're well enough, leave London. Go to
this address in Dorchester and ask for Mrs
Amelia Brock. She'll help you settle there.
Just show her this card.

He watches her drink and fall into painless sleep. DISSOLVE TO:
An hour later, when he departs, she's already looking healthier.
The nuns are astonished.

#86 EXT. LONDON STREETS. CHEAPSIDE – DAY

The pickpocket closes on NILS, but also witnesses NILS give
serious money to a homeless family and rescue a small dog from
a trio of street children tormenting it.

NILS

Stop tormenting that poor animal.
Remember boys, "Do as you would be done
by" like Charles Kingsley said.. Hurting
defenceless creatures diminishes us...

They regard him as if he's an alien as this thought's clearly never
entered their heads.
CLOSE ON The young pickpocket's listening and now in two
minds about robbing him. Old habits die hard though: NILS is
awake up and grabs the boy's wrist. A watching Bobby hurries
towards them.

NILS SALSTROM

The Bobby's seen you. Take this money -
FOR YOUR FAMILY, and for God's sake
stop stealing.

The amazed thief grins and bolts into the crowd.

BOBBY (YELLING)
Stop that dirty little blighter

The overweight Policeman gives up as the boy disappears into a rabbit warren of lanes and alleys full of whores and cut-throats. The Bobby looks for Nils but he's gone too.

#87 EXT. BRITISH MUSEUM - DAY.

NILS stands before the British Museum looking disturbed by the swelling numbers of uniformed army officers distributing enlistment forms to naively eager young men.

#88 INT. BRITISH MUSEUM JULY 1914 - DAY.

He sits at a long shiny cedar table poring over a pile of heavy musty books with a magnifying glass. Several dissolves show he's been at it for a while. At the end of the table is a white bearded curmudgeonly ACADEMIC MAN who glances at NILS disapprovingly over his pince-nez.
A beautiful upper-class WOMAN (full figured, brunette, fine clothes) catches his eye when she sits opposite. The old man approves of her. She and NILS make eye contact for a second and there's instant attraction. She smiles coyly and returns to her reading. He loses concentration for a moment. He now studies flora and woodland paintings of the Americas and JOHN GLOVER's Tasmanian flora and woodlands prints. The CURMUDGEON watches Nils like a hawk as Nils and the woman smile at each other again. NILS looks about to speak to her when the old man sees NILS' hands start to quiver as he excitedly examines something through the magnifying glass.
ECU: The page shows myriad kinds of woodland ferns. The map in the corner of the page indicates Georgia and Alabama.
When he produces the last withered leaf of "His" plant and checks it against the American drawing, they almost match. He looks longingly at the woman, now reading and then scans the huge room furtively and disregards all consequences, by removing a page from each book and pocketing them. Suddenly the old man's shuffling towards him so NILS pulls out a snuff box, which he

95

opens. The WOMAN's shocked at witnessing what he's done. The OLDER MAN's suddenly staring down at NILS trying find his voice and shaking in outrage.

> ACADEMIC MAN (HOARSE WHISPER)
> Why you're a damned vandal sir. This book's priceless. What you' ve done is sacrilege. Disgraceful

NILS mouths "sorry" at the woman and at the old man as he blows snuff into his face, inducing a sneezing attack, and incapacitating him. NILS stands and helps him into a chair and the woman watches in astonishment and disappointment as NILS hurries out of the reading room towards the entrance.

OLD MAN (SNEEZING, DISTRESSED)

Blast and damnation! Someone stop that vandal. Call the police! He's assaulted me. Help me.

Security guards come to his aid but NILS is gone.

#89 EXT. BRITISH MUSEUM – DAY

TRACKING - He leaps down the steps losing himself in a crowd of excited recruits watching a marching pipe band. Nils has a sudden vision of passing callow youth exiting a trench on the Western Front and being shot in the head before tumbling backwards, dead. NILS closes his eyes in horror as the young soldier looks at him weirdly.

#90 INT.BANK OF ENGLAND – DAY

NILS looks furious with himself, Inside the Bank of England he withdraws a great deal of cash and gold from a safety deposit box and places it in a Naval bag.

#91 INT.GENTLEMAN'S CLUB ON THE STRAND - DAY.

His face shows he's at another cross roads. He drinks heavily, resigned to whatever may come.

#92 EXT. UP-MARKET KNIGHTSBRIDGE.NILS'MANSION. DAY

NILS changes and packs a few clothes, some priceless jewels, gold and small paintings by Velazquez and De La Tour into a large canvas bag. Before leaving the house he studies it pensively as if for the last time.

#93 EXT. PALL MALL – DAY

NILS wanders alone aimlessly in the city, looking downcast and introspective, sipping whiskey from a large hip flask.

#94 EXT. HYDE PARK – DAY

MOVING - NILS approaches small crowd as he crosses a park. He's drunk as he listens to pro war speakers.

> ### SERGEANT (38,TALL,SOLID, MOUSTACHE)
> ..and the Empire needs you today like never before. The brutality of The German Hun is daily proven: days ago they bayoneted innocent women and children in Belgium on our very doorstep. I exhort all men of eligible age to Sign up today. The War Department is positive this will be a short

> ### SERGEANT CONT
> War and be over in three months
> ...POSITIVE they are!

Nils recklessly jumps onto the dais next to the Sergeant and eye-balls him intimidatingly.

NILS
Now what's that famous definition of the word "POSITIVE"? That's right: To be mistaken at the top of one's voice!

There's laughter and cries for him to "get off".

NILS
This soldier's spouting the same lies told by
warmongers through-out history. This War
won't be over in three months. Or three
years either.

The crowd shout at him and each other: "I concur";
"Lies" and "liar", POLTROON! and "Coward". NILS now
recognizes the WOMAN from the library in the crowd. She
pouts at him judgement-ally. But the attraction's still there.
The SERGEANT's sizing NILS up for a fight but thinks
better of it.

NILS
I was a soldier once and know this conflict
will be like no other.

MAN 1
Poppy cock! There were no Scandinavians
fighting in the Boer War or the Sudan.
You're not even English.

MAN 2
You've no business telling us anything...and
you're drunk!

NILS
I AM a British citizen. Not the Boer War or
the ..er, I fought at...I was wounded at er

There's an instant outburst of laughter. He might have just lost
everyone in his audience.

MAN 2

Tha's right... ..wounded in the brain! It's You
who's spinning lies mate. Whoppers! Which
War if not those Wars? The Crimean War
of 1854? Makin' you more'n 80 years old.
Yer do look like shite though. LAUGHTER
ENCOURAGES HIM Or maybe he killed
hundreds working as a short order cook in
the Catering Corps!

MORE LAUGHTER. NILS has lost them. Or has he?

NILS

Only the dead have seen the end of war you
Ninny!

What would you know of the reign of lead
or the lore of bayonets and their stomach
slitting ways - what in Hell's

name would YOU know of the glaze-eyed
gaze of a comrade exhaling his last mortal
breath.!

The man's silenced. There's a momentary hush. They all know
Nils has seen it all. He's convincing and the Army recruiters are
worried. The woman watches him intently.

But all past wars are child's play to this
Evil promise. Today's weapons will be as
threshing machines through wheat. In the
battle for Flanders Fields will fall the flower
of European youth..

Many dismayed faces start to share his terrible vision. NILS eyes
and the WOMAN'S eyes lock. They realize it's almost love at first
sight. She's very like a much younger paler version of Rowena. An
officer on the fringe gives a signal. Tough Military Police try to
force their way towards the dais. Some young Office workers want

101

Nils to continue and block their way.

NILS

These angry bitter old men will start this war but never fight it. Do NOT SIGN your own death warrants for the bloody arrogance OF Empire!!ARMAGEDDON is come.

The OFFICER has heard enough and gives a signal.

OFFICER

Bloody traitor. That's sedition you spineless coward! Arrest him!

An all in melee now breaks out. Some soldiers try to haul him off the dais, but he's a handful even though drunk. More police arrive and he belts a couple of them and takes to his heels. The woman follows him at a distance and after a mile sees him duck into a club. She's breathless as she enters the place a few minutes later. DISSOLVE TO

#95 INT.CLUB. THE WALPOLE AND BEEF. 1914 DAY

NILS sits in a quiet corner drinking coffee. The woman approaches him somewhat breathless

ELIZABETH (COQUETTISH)
Quite the versatile entertainer NILS SALSTROM - book vandal, thief, demagogue, musician, runner. Now add pugilist to that Curriculum vitae. I wonder when you might ever find time to sleep. I'm Lady ELIZABETH GAINES. But plain ELIZABETH to you.

NILS (CHASTENED, BEMUSED)
There's nothing plain about you!

But you already know my name and followed
me here??

(ELIZABETH smiles. He's surprised when she sits opposite him
and he signals the waiter for more coffee).
> You saw what I did. Yet you're here and
> talking civilly to me.

ELIZABETH
Are you like Lord Byron? Mad, bad and
dangerous to know? I recognized you
from a violin concerto you gave at Covent
garden last year. I liked what I heard. And
what I saw. When I heard you speak I knew
you must have had reasons for the library
outrage.

(She touches his hand unconsciously smelling his pheromones).
> You'll be page 1 news in "The Times"
> tomorrow. Any plans?

NILS
How is it that a woman like you is
unattached?

ELIZABETH
I was married. It was arranged, loveless.
It suited our parents. But he was old and
dropped off the perch of course. No children
is a regret however.

NILS
But you're still young..not too late.

ELIZABETH

38? Not so young! My guess

is they'll cite you as the instigator of that
riot. Bring sedition charges.

I'm astounded you're casually sitting here
while some artist's likeness will have you
identified you by name by the morning. You
may, however, stay with me...for a time...if
You like.

NILS

Are you quite certain? That's uncommon
generosity Elizabeth. It.. would just be for a
few days - till I can find passage on the kind
of America-bound cargo ship whose captain
doesn't inspect passports closely. I WAS
merely exercising my right to free speech you
realize...back In the park.

ELIZABETH

It was inflammatory. Your convict-ions are
impressive, but were recklessly put.

(She writes something and gives it to him)
I want to help you. I'll leave now and suggest
you do so soon. Come after dark. Maybe it's
not protocol, but these are strange times.
Who knows what travails the future may
bring.

#96 INT.ELIZABETH'S TUDOR ERA HOUSE BEDROOM.
NIGHT

He's admitted in the back door under cover of darkness and she
ushers him up to her room, where he stows his gear. A young an-

gular looking maid with a severe haircut watches them climb the stairs with a disapproving look.

#97 INT.DINING ROOM – NIGHT

They sit finishing a nice dinner and study each other wordlessly for a minute before she offers him her hand and leads him upstairs. She disrobes provocatively as she closes the bedroom door after them and they come together and make wild and passionate love.

#98 IN. UPSTAIRS BEDROOM – MORNING

They're naked and wrapped in each other's arms.

ELIZABETH
That was just lovely. All of it. Well you're certainly the complete Renaissance man. Is there any instrument you can't play?

NILS

Hmm. Doubt I'd get a decent note out of a
Swahili nose pipe, but I could probably play
chopsticks on your nipples with my tongue if
you like. Truth is, you leave me speechless.

ELIZABETH

That's difficult to believe. Perhaps you need
another dais.

They laugh and embrace and he enters her again

ELIZABETH

I have to say,I could fall madly in lust with
you. Whatever would the Suffragette Mrs
Pankhurst say if she heard me say that?

NILS

Probably something like "make hay and
love while the sun shines". I haven't felt this
happy since I can remember, Elizabeth.

ELIZABETH

You never married? But you must have
known true love?

He rolls onto his side and studies her face

NILS

In worst times I sought the company of
sad women of the night. But there were too
many demons and torments to dally with
a woman of..substance. But that's a foolish
statement as life starts with the random
chance of birth right. So 'twas a soldier's
span for me, and that and the solitary life are
most of what I've known since childhood,
when my family were killed.

(Her empathetic loving looks say it all)
> Music's been my constant companion and
> salvation. I never shared these thoughts with
> a living soul.

She embraces him tightly and they make love again.

#99 EXT. AUTOBUS STOP IN SUBURBAN LONDON – DAY

Elizabeth gets off an "antique" autobus and turns a corner into Cornwell St, where Nils' house is. She sees police at his garden gate and in an upstairs window. She returns to her house with a copy of "The Times" and NILS is a feature story, his true identity revealed.

#100   INT. ELIZABETH'S HOUSE. NIGHT 1914

NILS
> I can't hide here after tomorrow - it'll
> jeopardize your entire situation. Though in
> truth I could imagine

> sharing a wonderful life with you Elizabeth.
> Chance told me to head for America,and
> disappear till after this War. It seems stupid
> asking..

She knows exactly what he's going to ask.

#101   EXT. AN OLD FREIGHTER AT LONDON DOCKS.
NIGHT

A taxi idles at the docks, the back door open. There's a cargo ship loading in the background. Elizabeth and Nils walk hand in hand towards the gangway, the taxi driver watches them intuitively. She hugs and kisses Nils. He's strangely desperate.

NILS
I don't want to leave you. Not ever!

ELIZABETH
Neither do I. Stay here in England. Don't go.
Just don't..

They kiss passionately while at the top of the gangplank a sailor
whistles for Nils to board the ship. It's secretive

NILS
It's too risky for you. I'll write you. And
often.

ELIZABETH
As will I

#102 EXT.SHIP.LONDON DOCKS.NIGHT

She watches tearfully as he hurries into the fog half hiding the freighter and is smuggled on board the Venezuelan ship. He notes the crew are clearly a dangerous lot.

#103 EXT. FREIGHTER ON JET BLACK SEA NIGHT. 1914

NILS looks bereft standing at the stern and shines a match on a photograph of a younger ELIZABETH dressed for a special occasion. CU as he stares at the mounting waves and spume despairing and empty. FADE TO BLACK.CUT TO:

#104 INT. CLASSROOM. WICKLOW HIGH 2027 DAY.

Fade in stark light. Back in the present the loud bell wakes Alex from his fit and he sits shaking slightly as the students file out without permission. One female STUDENT notices his unusual demeanour and turns off the projector before approaching him.

GENEVIEVE
You don't look well Sir. Do you want me to call someone?

ALEX
I'll be okay in a minute. Thanks.

She nods but is unconvinced he's "okay". CUT TO:

#105 HOBART CLUB.AMATEURS'NIGHT.PRESENT

ALEX is performing. People there can't believe how good he is. He sees SIMON and ROWENA enter. The applause subsides

ALEX
Thanks. Er now I'd like to sing a new song written by Simon, the guy over there with the beautiful ROWENA...It's called SOMETIMES and I hope you like it as much as I do.

SIMON'S aghast and ecstatic. ROWENA's embarrassed.
He sings the Legionary song well and it's really well received.
There's total silence for a few seconds then enthusiastic applause.
It's moved them. ALEX waves for SIMON to stand up and take a
bow. There are tears in SIMON's eyes. ROWENA looks at ALEX
with absolute love.
ALEX joins his friends in the corner. SIMON's elated and a
couple of baby boomer women close by who invite him over to
join their table. ROWENA snuggles up to ALEX as they watch
a Cowboy type play a HANK WILLIAMS Country and Western
song. In the darkness the music stirs a traumatic memory and
again ALEX lapses into a brief catatonic state while ROWEAN
obliviously leans on his shoulder. CLOSE on ALEX's staring eyes.
FADE TO:

SUPER A L A B A M A U.S.A 1 9 6 5

#106 EXT. HIGH SUSPENSION BRIDGE OVER RAGING
RIVER - DAY

From the lofty tree POV of a squirrel peering through foliage, a
MAN, his back to the animal, stands precariously at the edge of
a metal stanchion jutting out over a raging river far below, his
arms outstretched as if tempting fate. ZOOM POV shows NILS
(ALEX) staring blankly out into nothingness. He looks to be on
drugs, very drunk or has found his preferred method of suicide.
A car, driven by two late twenties "Rednecks", one in a cowboy
hat, pulls up on the bridge for a minute before crossing it. There's
loud music issuing from the car radio.
The Rednecks realize he's totally legless drunk, as he's swaying
perilously on the parapet. The DRIVER has a flat top hairstyle
and a dumb aggressive face. He laughs at NILS and calls out

REDNECK
Hey you hopeless booze hound! Why don't you
just jump, you legless long-haired hippie freak.

NILS suddenly finds a reason not to jump and vaults over the bridge railing to confront his abuser.

NILS
How can I jump if I'm legless? That's a tautology you DIXIEMORON!

The passenger opens his window and hurls a bottle of beer at NILS' head, but NILS catches it and pitches it back so hard it shatters their windscreen. The driver panics as NILS sprints towards the car and it roars off. He yells after them and then collapses in an alcoholic stupor heightened by his coughing attack.

#107 EXT. SOUTH COUNTRY TOWN - MORNING.

PANNING:It's a sunny day as CAMELIA, a verdant but feral-looking Deep South town begins to "wake up". An occasional beat-up old Dodge or Buick cruises down "Main" Street towards the new Wal Mart on the edge of town. A tobacco chewing good old boy walking a Doberman stops to chat across a garden fence to an elderly couple. Next door two pre teens play baseball in the now-stark sunlight.

#108 EXT. ALABAMA COUNTRY ROAD EDGED BY WOODS - DAY.

WIDE - A long stretch of country road is empty apart from a a solitary new Cadillac parked on the verge at a distance. From a MLS POV a man can be partly seen standing in front of the car urinating. It's Nils and he's looking distinctly unwell once more. He suddenly collapses over the bonnet for a minute before somehow climbing onto it. He studies the page he stole from the British Library and scans the area with binoculars, focusing on a small stream at a cutting under the road a half mile away. He is engrossed when a bus full of black and white Civil Rights Freedom Riders – young blacks and whites roars by. Some of the young students give him peace signs and he makes the V for victory sign.
Moments later an old VW Kombie with audible and visible engine trouble drives into view. The painted sign on the Kombie reads "End Racial Tyranny. Equal Rights for All Americans Now". It passes him and pulls onto the verge a little further along. Two young twenties white Hippie males get out (JOHN and CHARLIE both long haired and in paisley and leather) with LORETTA, a young African American. She's very black and buxom, in full Afro hairstyle.

LORETTA
Hi Dude...do you know where we can find a
gas station in this hick bayou?

NILS

Sure. Camellia's only another five clicks and
there's a mechanic there..but I wouldn't go
using the word "Hick" too freely round here
if I were you...

LORETTA

Oh yeah? I'll try to bite my tongue
sometimes then, if, like you say, we've
entered the Twilight Zone.

NILS

Worse! It's backwoods Alabama! Better bite
it often and bite it hard.

She's taken aback and indicates to the boys he's an odd ball when
she heads back to the van. ON THEM. In the complacency of
their youth they merely grin and wave as they depart. He watches
them, worried. DISSOLVE TO

#109 EXT.ALABAMA FOREST.DAY

In the woods Nils is once more on hands and knees coughing glob-
ules of congealed blood as he crawls towards a brook. He searches
the long grass along the river bank and is suddenly ecstatic and starts
singing and coughing simultaneously when he sees the same little
fern of antiquity. In a delirious state he pulls off some fronds and
starts wolfing them down. DISSOLVE TO
Later in the day he's looking much better and healthier as he glances
in a small mirror he holds. The plant is working its magic but when
he looks at his reflection he is suddenly bereft: for no apparent reason
he bows his head and starts to weep. The weeping grows into a gut-
tural-deep-sobbing and shoulder-wrenching grief.

#110 EXT. CAMELIA ALABAMA.DUSK

As the day wanes a dramatically younger, healthier NILS drives into
Camellia to celebrate with a beer and a meal. He parks opposite a gas
station work shop in the town square and grimaces as he watches a
mechanic working under the hood of the Kombie.
Nils is casually dressed as he strolls the forty metres across the road
towards the town's only bar. On a long wooden bench stretched along
the raised veranda of this place, a suspect and thuggish looking quar-
tet of semi drunk "Good Old Boys" swig from bottles of Budweiser.
They're an accident waiting to happen.
CLOSE - The bar's name, "The White Camelia", is advertised by an
"ancient" red and yellow neon sign WHICH starts to flash above the
men's heads as night thickens. A savage yellow dog sits at the foot of
the apparent leader of these men, and a hunting rifle leans against the
wooden wall behind him. Nils is clearly not welcome.

NILS (BEST SOUTHERN ACCENT)
Evenin' fellers. Nice night..

He doesn't finish and is taken aback when he notices a Sheriff's
badge on one of these nasties, and a holstered gun under his shirt.
The SHERIFF grunts aggressively. One of the others spits phlegm
near NILS' boot.

#111 EXT/INT.WHITE CAMELIA BAR. NIGHT

NILS glances over his shoulder as he enters the brightly lit bar and sees the sheriff glaring at him through the window.

FROM THE POV of the students seen earlier and now sitting at a table NILS heads for the counter and orders a meal and a beer. He skim views the clientele in concern and is worried when the three young Freedom Riders wave to him. When he approaches them they're stunned by his appearance as while he's wearing the same clothes, he looks twenty years younger!

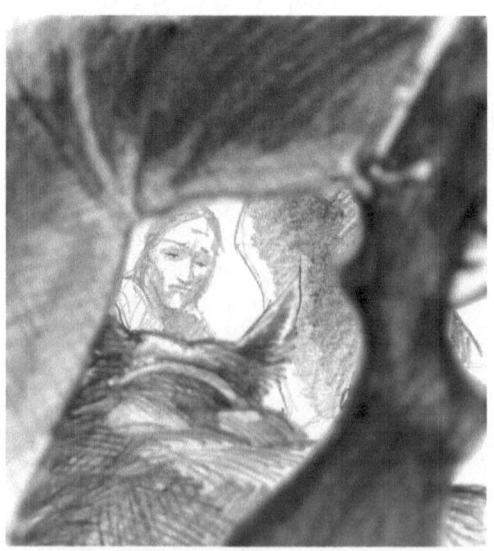

#112 EXT.WHITE CAMELIA BAR.NIGHT

Back on his bench the Sheriff opens another bottle of Budweiser with his teeth and skulls it down.

SHERIFF HARRY DORFMANN
Judas Priest! What the fuck's this world's comin' to when two city faggots and a coon bitch think they c'n jist walk into the bar ai love and drink Bud jes' like any common folk.

DEPUTY JACKSON
Yeah, just like they own this place!

SHERIFF DORFMANN

It really pisses me off, close to boilin' point. Got me feelin' like a servin' 'v Pinko and Nigra spare ribs...?

117

DEPUTY ANDY LEE(LAUGHING APPROVAL)
Right on Harry.

SHERIFF DORFMANN
Might even be a good night for a little clan reunion...

They look up at the starless night and fall silent.

#113 INT. KNIGHTS BAR CAMELIA ALABAMA - NIGHT.

The mood inside is threatening. There's a juke box, a Confederate flag over the bar and prints of old sideshow paintings of Annie Oakley, ROBERT E LEE, BUFFALO BILL and Chief Sitting Bull. In a corner there's pool table where four early twenties red-neck males are arguing aggressively, seemingly about the students. The "Yankee Hippies" seem naively oblivious to all the threatening looks their presence is eliciting. NILS is visibly concerned and reluctantly joins them. CHARLIE, (22, skinny, long haired, John Lennon glasses) is talkative.

CHARLIE
I think we mighta met your father earlier Dude. He was maybe even wearing the same clothes?

NILS
Yeah, sure. My dad was out on the road. Listen I don't want to sound alarmist, but it's dangerous here for you guys. Haven't you noticed the looks you're all getting here?

LORETTA
Why are you trying to scare us Man? We've done nothing wrong. We're Freedom Riders sure, but we're also Peaceniks minding our own sweet business.

NILS (SHAKING HIS HEAD)

Seriously? I'm sorry to tell you but this is the
Deep South, not New York. In the local patois,
your Constitutional Rights count for Diddly
Squat! You can't afford naivety down here. Did
that Sheriff say anything when you arrived.

Their looks show they're scared of him.

If your Kombie's cactus, let me drive you
to the city now. Get you on a plane back to
wherever you all come from. Those good old
boys getting plastered on beer on the porch
are an accident waiting to happen.

CHARLIE

You're freakin' me Man. That van's my
brother's. I can't just leave it here! The
Mechanic assured us it'd be ready by eight
(regards his watch)5 minutes ago.

He looks around and gets apprehensive.

Let's go guys

NILS

Head for the gas station now. I'll follow in
a minute. Whatever you do when you pass
those men on the stoop..do not let them bait
you. Say nothing. No matter what!

LORETTA (ANGRY,HURT)

But we've got rights! This is our country too.

NILS

I'm sorry Darlin', but down here it might as
well be 1865, not 1965. Here you've only got
the rights they tell you you've got.

#114 INT/EXT.CAMELIA BAR.

The three get up and walk quietly and self consciously out the door and past the good old boys, who're now quite "liquored up". NILS strolls to open the door and listens and watches unseen by the men on the verandah.

SHERIFF(HE'S FRIGHTENING)
Well lookee what we got here: some piss ant
city hippies and their nigger bitch to keep
'em knee deep in charcoal pussy.
UnEEversITY educated Piss ants Come
down here with your Equal rights, end Jim
Crow laws placards.. tell us Southern folks
how to live our lives. That uppity nigger
Martin Luther King needs a goddam rocket
up his black ass..an a one way ticket back t'
his beloved Africa!

DEPUTY JACKSON
Damn straight Harry. Ship thet GollyWog
back t' Liberia with them other spear
chuckers!

LORETTA'S a fiery girl and simultaneously fighting tears and
rage. She fatally stops walking for a moment, about to "lose it"
before CHARLIE grabs her arm and pulls her along.

JOHN (WHISPERING)
Don't listen to him Loretta. He doesn't know
shit from Shinola. Just keep walking. Don't..

They're half way across the street now. The mechanic's by the
Kombie. He gives them the thumbs up - it's ready. The Sheriff is
off his seat and stepping down onto the road from the veranda, a
powerful rifle in his hands.

SHERIFF DORFFMANN
Did I just detect an act of dumb insolence
you Bitch? Hold it right there dipshits. Ah
got some important advice fer y'all..fore you
depart these environs toute suite..

They stop in their tracks, uncertain. The sheriff's cronies step
down onto the road. Nils flinches as the sheriff saunters towards
them malevolently.

SHERIFF
Now JEMIMA..or is it TOPSY..?

He's a monster and grabs her breast with one hand and tries for
her crotch. It's terrifying. She's weeping and the boys are para-
lyzed with fear. Nils steps onto the road. Charlie suddenly lurches
forward, and shoves the Sheriff away from her but immediately
whacks the youth across the head with his rifle. Blood spurts
from the wound.

121

DORFFMANN

You really shouldn'a done that BOY. That's
the Goddamn-est dumbest thing you ever
did you Yankee son of a bitch.

CHARLIE struggles on his knees but the Sheriff kicks him in the
stomach. He gets gingerly to his feet and joins his friends. The three
huddle cowering twenty metres from the Sheriff as Nils appears and
steps between them. The Sheriff and deputy are in a dangerous mood.

NILS (PLACATING)

Maybe I can be of some assistance here
Sheriff. My young friends meant no offence
I assure you..they're good citizens really.
I do think this boy needs some medical.
help though. I can pay their fine if they've
broken any rules. Get them out of your hair.
And get him to a (NILS CONT) clinic in
Montgomery. I'm sure they didn't mean to
mess up here.

NILS slightly diverts his fury for a moment but the alcohol takes
over again and he gestures at Nils with his rifle.

SHERIFF DORFFMANN

A'hm only gonna say this the once you
Goddam Peckerwood. Mind Yur own fuck'n
business and get the Hell outta my town now
or suffer a world 'a hurt. As fer you Yankee
maggots ah'm gonna give you one hour to
vamoose outa my goddamn county or arrest
your sorry asses for disturbin' the peace,
speedin' in a Nazi ve-hICAL, spittin', foul
language, an night jaywalkin'or whatever ah
damn-well see fit. Are we on the same page
maggots? Are You gettin' mah continental
drift?"

(They nod hard).

CHARLIE (PAINFULLY)
Does..does that...mean we can leave Sheriff.
Now?

SHERIFF
Jesus wept but you're one dumb sonvabitch
boy? Git the fuck outta CAMELIA now and
don't take yer foot off the gas pedal till you
reach the state line! And you..

Peckerwood! You're still here when ah
distinctly remember dismissin' you a
minute ago BOY.! (TO NILS)

(He lifts the gun barrel at Nils and then swings it to point at NILS'
car).

SHERIFF

Now git! And Git fast fore I get really pissed.!

NILS makes eye contact with the kids telling them to go fast and
as he turns to hurry off himself. Nils jogs for his car and starts
it up and the kids drive off in the opposite direction. The sheriff
watches Nils drives his Caddy out of town.

#115 EXT.OUTSKIRTS OF CAMELIA ALABAMA.NIGHT

As soon as he is out of eyeshot Nils pulls in along the verge and
visibly reflects on what's just happened. Several times he looks to
and from the road ahead and then back whence he's just come.
He now does a U Turn and drives back slowly with his lights off
and parks in behind a hedge just outside of town. He leaps out
and runs back 250 metres to the town through the back lanes of
Main Street houses, sprinting fast and silently.
He hides behind a barber shop front and watches as the Sheriff

and his cronies drink on into the night. Two hours pass and the bar shuts down and he looks ready to head on his way when the mechanic suddenly emerges from the darkness with a crate of beer. The Sheriff pats the mechanic on the back. Nils looks compelled to stay now. The cronies sit around for an hour and then stand and look back at the way the students' Kombie went. NILS' face shows he now knows what's afoot.

FROM HIS POV, hidden among tall bushes Nils watches the road for a minute until two beat up old pickup trucks pass by within thirty metres of his position. A minute later he starts his near noiseless engine and drives slowly after the trucks, his lights turned off. FADE TO BLACK:

#116 INT. HOBART HOSPITAL WARD. PRESENT NIGHT 2027

FADE IN: Through the open door of a ward Rowena's watches an attractive young 30's (blonde, gold earings, expensive haircut) female Doctor examining a comatose Alex. A male Dr the same age (shaved head, goatee, earring) brushes past Rowena carrying X-Rays. She's stunned by the X-Rays. They lift his gown to examine and confer on his many old wounds.

DR MARGRIT ASH

My God! These wounds are consistent with life ending

sword and bullet wounds. And look at those cicatrices. Who the heck is this guy, the Count of Monte bloody Christo?

DR JIM ALLAN (INCREDULOUS)

His biggest worry isn't catatonic fits either! Margrit - when was the last time you saw a case of TB as advanced as this on anyone but a CORPSE? Whatever.. Action Man here's time's almost up? Is that his wife out there

They look towards an apprehensive ROWEAN. Dr ASH gives ALEX an adrenaline shot and he suddenly regains consciousness. The DOCTORS regard him as if he's from another planet as he starts to dress.

#117 INT. ALEX'S UNIT – NIGHT 2027

ROWEAN arrives at ALEX's unit to move in. She's struggling with a suitcase and a box of bric-a-brac as he opens the door. She's astounded. It's beautiful and opulent inside.

> ### ROWENA
> ALEX SELKIRK. My God! Your flat! How? These are the trappings of a multi millionaire. So why... exactly, does a filthy rich and catflap European emigre need to work as a lowly paid music teacher when you've got all this?

She spins in a circle, disbelieving. He's uncomfortable.

> ### ROWENA
> This is all too weird Alex You're starting to scare me now. I guess I asked for.
>
> it...but you didn't totally prepare me either.

He puts the box down and embraces her.

> ### ALEX
> Since we've reached the point of no return, my real name's not ALEX SELKIRK, it's NILS SALSTROM. I was born in Copenhagen..well before the 1952 it says on my passport, too.

> ### ROWENA (APPREHENSIVELY SOFT)
> HOW long before 1952 ALEX?

> ALEX
> A while. Will that do for now?

She's clearly imagining all kinds of things now
> The thing is, if you trust me and love me a
> little as you say you do, maybe nothing else
> matters

She nods slowly and lays her head on his shoulder.

#118 INT. ALEX'S UNIT DAY/NIGHT 2027

A SERIES OF DISSOLVES REVEALING DOMESTICITY AND
THE CLOSENESS OF THEIR BOND.
They are like a young loving couple. ROWENA's transformed and
at her very best. As is ALEX. DISSOLVE TO

#119 EXT.WICKLOW HIGH.DAY

ALEX heads to the teachers' car-park to get something from his car
and finds faeces smeared over his windscreen and finds two tyres
slashed. He's angry but resignedly heads back to the school junior
yard. As he rounds the corner of A Block he sees a group of younger kids staring and pointing in fear at a third floor window and he
immediately bursts into a break neck sprint.
From his sprinting POV, two gorilla masked seniors are holding
a uniformed youth by his ankles and threatening to drop him on
the cement 30 feet below. Alex has covered a lot of ground and he's
exploding with effort, but it's to no avail as they let the body go. He
slows and misses a step as he raises his hands to his face in despair.
He trips and rolls, hurting his shoulder in the process. ALEX leaps
to his feet again and sprints to the still body on the cement, groaning in despair.
He hears laughter from behind him as he reaches the youth but
is shocked and then relieved to find it's just a store MANNIKIN
dressed in a Wicklow uniform. He turns to find about a dozen
senior boys are laughing at him. They've set him up, but he looks
furiously up at the window, and despite pain and bleeding arms,
runs flat out into the block to the top of the staircase and past

many rooms glancing in each as he runs.

There's a race through the building, but they escape into the seniors' court yard full of milling 17 and 18 year- olds just before he can catch them. Many seniors are decent and like him, but it's clear they're in the thrall of the surly thuggish looking group of eight, standing in a knot to one side. Several smirk at him and the others glare confrontation-ally. He approaches three sports jock types in the group, while struggling to hide how sick he feels and looks.

ALEX:

Any of you see three seniors just run out
here from that Exit in the last 20 seconds? In
masks?

They shrug at him with "we know nothing" looks. He walks through the crowd looking at faces and checks out two garbage bins. Inside one he finds two ape masks which he fishes out and holds up. He glances contemptuously at the thug group, but there's only silence and insolence.

#120 INT. PARENT TEACHER MEETING - NIGHT

ON JASON. In the School Hall it's Parent Teacher night and JASON loses it when he sees his ex-wife with her new partner. ALEX watches him with a look of concern. CUT TO
ALEX looks up to the line of parents waiting and notices the marginalized RAELENE with her parents. They're dirt poor and clearly doing it tough. ALEX stands to greet them and visibly surprises the hard man father with the strength of his handshake. RAELENE's apprehensive.

ALEX

Hello Mr and Mrs BARLOW, g'day
RAELENE. Glad you could all make it on
such a bitterly cold night.

ANDY BARLOW

So, how's she goin', our girl?

ALEX

I have to say I was pretty worried about
RAELENE when I first arrived here. Bu--
ut, Im really chuffed to be able to tell you
she's now turned the corner and starting to
realize

ALEX

some of her true potential. (RAELENE perks
up). And I'm absolutely elated to be able to
tell that while her voice is untrained, it's got
a beautiful timbre to it and it could actually
take her places. If she started coming
to lunch-time practice regularly I can
guarantee good results.. It's not compulsory
though. Her decision entirely.

RAELENE's fighting the onset of totally unfamiliar emotions, her
looks never softer. Her parents are beaming.

FATHER

Well thanks mate. That's real good to hear.

ALEX

You're very welcome. My name's ALEX, by
the way

Her dad gratefully shakes his hand again before they leave. From
his POV they both pat her shoulders approvingly and Raelene
half turns to look back at him before they exit the hall. It's a look
of appreciation, respect and admiration she's never offered a
teacher before. CUT TO
Another couple of parents sit as ALEX spots JASON leaving the
Hall sneaking swigs from a hip flask. ALEX notices the growing
line of impatient parents by Jason's desk and when he sees JASON
walk in eyeballing his ex and her partner he knows what's happened.

ALEX

I'm sorry but I have to duck outside for a
minute..one of the students will bring you
both coffee.

#121 INT/EXT SCHOOL CAR-PARK. NIGHT

They're fine with it. He hurries after Jason, and leads him to the
carpark. Carl also notices and follows them. Alex makes a Mobile
call for a taxi.

ALEX

Give me the flask JASON. You've made real
progress. Don't ruin your life tonight over
one bloody setback. Don't piss it all away.
Just go home now. Watch "EXTRAS". Smile.
Go to sleep. Tomorrow's another day.

JASON (FIGHTING TEARS)

They're humiliating me showing up like that
together. They're my kids, not that Bastard's!
Who the Hell's he think he is? I'm gonna
give that smug prick a hiding..

ALEX

No one commits Hara Kiri on my watch but
me. I've called you a taxi

The cab arrives and ALEX leads JASON to it and shoves him into
the back.

ALEX

Mate, just drop him at 121 Athol St Sandy
Bay please. Nowhere else! Wait till he's gone
inside and you can keep the rest of the $50
okay?

129

Carl follows him back into the building talking to him of of hearing.

#122 INT SCHOOL HALL FOYER WICKLOW - NIGHT.

> ALEX
> I said he's fine. Well, I mean, no actually he's
> in bad shape. But..look, his wife's in there
> with her new lover. Give the guy a break
> CARL. I know you're not really the mean
> spirited misery guts some people say you are
> and you pretend to be.

CARL is gob-smacked, but only for a second. As he watches Alex go Carl has a perceptible change of heart.

#123 INT. WICKLOW SCHOOL HALL.END OF TERM BREAKUPDAY

The whole school's there, impatient for their holidays..
DAMIEN, GRETEL, SALLY, RAELENE and ALEX come on stage and do a wonderful rendition of the song and the audience response is terrific, apart from the exceptions the bullies CHAD and WAYNE and some of their evil senior mates, who all look livid at the talents of shy children. Chad and Wayne confer with three much bigger senior students and the construct is menacing. Meanwhile the performers beam with pleasure at the response and leave the stage as the bell rings for break up. Nils is shaken for a second though when he spies a senior in a ski mask among the exiting throng, who turns and makes a raised fist at Alex before disappearing in the crowd.

#124 INT. SCHOOL HALL – DAY

Behind the curtain GRETEL, RAELENE, and SALLY approach ALEX and give him the kind of loving hugs daughters would give a beloved father. DAMIEN grins and shakes his hand. The four teens are transformed.

GRETEL
Um, Mr "SELKY", we all just want to say
thanks. Thanks for all that you've done for
us.

Thanks for caring. Um, we got you this. It's
not much.

She hands him a small wrapped gift and card and they smile at
him as they leave.

SALLY
Have a great break Mr SELKY. You are
coming back aren't you? We need you. We
all do.

He's having trouble swallowing and visibly fighting long forgotten
emotions. CLOSE - As another teacher approaches, he kneels,
pretending to do up his shoe, but he's fighting back tears for the
third time in 200 years. Alone again he opens the envelope and
reads the card, which says
TO MR SELKIRK, A TERRIFIC TEACHER – AND OUR OTH-
ER DAD. WITH LOVE FROM YOUR KIDS, SALLY, GRETEL,
REALENE AND DAMIEN. THANK YOU AND HAPPY HOLI-
DAYS.
He now opens the small present and finds a chintzy little gold-co-
loured electric guitar. His face shows this cost something and
these kids are poor,. From the look on his face it's the best and
most important present he's ever received. It releases long hidden
memories. The tough guy ALEX's waterworks moment is saved
by the second siren and he wipes a single tear from his eye.

#125 EXT. HIGH PLAYGROUND – DAY

ALEX delegates a student to pack up his gear and goes on a
last schoolyard patrol before the holiday.
As he rounds the corner of the recreation block he comes
upon a shocking sight. Three sizeable seniors in the skull
masks are kicking the stuffing out of DAMIEN as he lies

tucked up in a ball on the asphalt sobbing. Another masked youth films it on his Mobile. Gretel and Sally are cowering nearby as another senior stands over MARTY who has clearly been hit, having come to his aid. Alex loses it for a few seconds and sprints the short distance to them so fast he's upon them, and a female PE teacher follows fast behind him clutching a First Aid kit. Alex forgets his duty of care for a second and shoves one of the bullies hard wrenching off the mask and sending him rolling onto the asphalt.

The second assailant attacks ALEX but cops a really hard open handed smack in the face as ALEX snatches off his mask too. The youth and the third assailant back, off, one clutching his cheek. ALEX now grabs the "cameraman's" wrist hard, making him cringe in pain, and wrenches the Mobile from his hand and the mask from his head. MEREDITH, a young PE teacher ministers to Damien behind these goings on.

> ALEX
>
> JESUS CHRIST! Leave that kid alone you
> bloody gutless cowards! How can you
> boys do this to him? And you, you worm...
> filming it for that bloody website! You're
> supposed to look after weaker kids...
> Jeezuz!!

ALEX fights for self control as the four circle him warily, fists raised. They aren't totally stupid though and aren't game to attack. One runs towards him with a swinging haymaker misses by a mile and he cowers as Alex steps fast towards him.

> LES
>
> You better give us back that Mobile phone
> Selkirk, you fuck'n cunt. Our old man's 'll do
> for you. They'll kill yer.

ALEX moves fast now and shoves two of them over, breaks the Mobile in half, throws it to the cement and stomps it to pieces.

ALEX

That's what your heroic little film is worth
boys. Keep behaving like this and you're
destined for the big boys' prison and you
won't get off with a smack over the wrist in
there. They play for keeps..

Behind them DAMIEN's in agony as MEREDITH attends to him,
and he's sobbing uncontrollably. As a group of other teachers hurry towards the scene, the bullies hurry off, calling him names and
giving him the one finger salute. JOHNNY, the nastiest of them
yells a threat.

BARRY SNOWDON

You bloody jerk of a teacher. We'll sue you..
after my old man beats seven shades of shit
out of yer. And my uncle's a cop, too, so
you're dead meat Selkirk.

Alex and the three kids kneel over Damien and Gretel cradles his
head. Alex is on his Mobile.

NILS

Hello, could you send an ambulance to
WICKLOW HIGH. Immediately please.
There's one on the way...ah okay thanks.

#126 INT. ADMIN BLOCK WICKLOW – DAY

It's close to dark as ALEX sits outside CARL's office looking
through the half open door. Inside several PARENTS stand arguing with CARL as well as a uniformed cop and another cop in a
suit whom he can't quite see.

#127 HOSPITAL WARD – NIGHT

ON DAMIEN - He's a mess. He has a wrist and an arm in plas-
ter, his eye-lids and cheeks are black and blue, he's doped up on
pain killers and he's obviously been bawling. ROWENA stands

next to the boy's mother, who's in shock and seated next to the bed. JASON and JENN stand on the other side of the bed next to GRETEL, SALLY and her mum.

GRETEL
We're so sorry DAIM. About what happened. I hate those boys. I've never hated anyone. But I hate them. And I hate that school.

DAMIEN
I I I'm n never g g g going b b back there. N n not e ever.

JASON and ROWEAN are worried about his state of mind.

#128 INT. HEADMASTER'S OFFICE - DUSK

Carl looks distressed. There's an ugly male parent with a broken nose in a blue boilermaker's suit. And Snowden's there too, with his brother in law WAL, the parent of one of the boys Alex "assaulted".

The other person is parent ERICA GALE, about 45, who's highly agitated and apparently just rushed over from COLES, as she's still in uniform. Outside the office a young earnest looking policeman leans against a foyer wall, keeping an eye on ALEX.

WAL PURVIS (TO CARL)
..and that bastard shouldn't be teachin' anywhere, ever! My boy WARREN's arm's fractured. I want your gutless teacher gaoled for what he done. An we're suin'. him an' the Education Department.

CARL(APPREHENSIVE)

Your son's 19 years old and no longer a
minor. He took part in a thuggish brutal
attack on a junior boy, with his identity
hidden by a horrible mask - a coward's
mask. Let me assure you he's in very serious
trouble. The victim's family could sue all of
your sons...and all of you..

They all look stunned by this possible prospect.

DETECTIVE SNOWDEN

That remains to be seen Mr FROBISHER.
We'll fully investigate the incident but
your teacher clearly assaulted three..er two,
minors in his charge. They are school kids,
so I'll be escorting him to the city lock up for
further questioning. You parents can leave
now.I'll take it from here.

(ASIDE WHISPER TO WAL) Believe me
mate when I tell you this bloke will get
what's coming to him.

CARL half hears his loaded words and glances at this menacing
Detective apprehensively as they all leave.

CARL(PHONING MESSAGE BANK)

ROWENA? It's CARL. I'm assuming you're
at the hospital. You need to ring me as soon
as possible. ALEX needs our help.

#129 EXT. WICKLOW HIGH.NIGHT

FROM CARL'S POV ALEX is aggressively "helped" into the back
of the Police vehicle and it drives off towards the city lights.

#130 POLICE STATION – NIGHT

MOVING. ALEX is walking through the old building almost wedged between SNOWDEN and two burly looking uniformed cops. A few other Cops glance up from paper work as they pass. A bored looking prostitute being interviewed by a cop at a desk watches him for a second with a slightly worried look. She "thinks" ALEX is in serious trouble as they walk down the corridor towards the "less populated" part of the old building.

> SNOWDEN
> So glad you could join us for the grand tour
> MIS-TER SELKIRK.I knew I'd be
>
> seeing you again, you cunt. And I also
> thought you'd appreciate seeing some of
> the Heritage features of the station ....it's
> the oldest cell in the country that's still in
> ...occasional use..

TRACKING. The sombre mood grows creepier as they descend several flights of old stone steps into the bowels of the building. At the bottom of the stairs is a small dank cell in a dark corner of the basement.

> SNOWDEN
> Yeah we all thought you deserved a close
> inspection of this particular "room". I read
> somewhere that in Europe they used to call
> these cells oubliettes. Do you know what that
> word means, Arsehole?

He's not mucking around. ALEX knows he's in real danger but can't help himself.

> ALEX/NILS
> I forget! Why don't you tell me,
> DUNDERKLUMPEN.

SNOWDEN

Ah we've got one king sized clever dick here
you Blokes. See, in the French language,
OUBLIETTE means a place to forget Oh, I'm
really gonna enjoy this!

These three bad cops are "savage dogs on
short leashes".

SNOWDEN opens the cell door and pushes ALEX in. They all
follow him in. SNOWDEN locks the door after them and pockets
the key.

SNOWDEN

Fancy yourself as a handyman with your
fists don'tcher?

Yeah, with kids maybe! And my nephew
was one of 'em. But

let's see you try it on with three physically
mature men.

ALEX (HE CAN'T HELP HIMSELF)
Three? I hope you're not counting yourself as
one of 'em Mister hippoPLODamous!

SNOWDEN's shaking with rage and bent on mayhem as he
removes his jacket, but ALEX doesn't wait and grabs him with his
arms still stuck in his half-removed jacket and spins him around
so he whacks into the other two Cops. Heads smack together as
he punches SNOWDEN in the throat and temporarily cripples
another with a kneecap kick.

The cell's too small to manoeuvre and he does the three of them
like a dinner. The fracas brings a half dozen OFFICERS running
down the stairs but they can't open the cell and don't have a spare
key. ALEX sits down on the bed with the three semi conscious
cops sprawled around him in various states of pain. ALEX ad-
dresses the other officers.

139

ALEX

I'm making a formal complaint to the
Ombudsman about Police brutality in this
station. I've been attacked by these three and
I demand I be allowed to call my Lawyer..

One of them is livid but can't get at him. A conscientious young
female OFFICER though hurries back upstairs for another key
and responsible assistance.

COP 1 (ICILY)

The only call you'll be making mate will
be to an orthopaedic surgeon when I finish
with you!

ALEX laughs out loud and the cop looks apoplectic.

#131 INT. POLICE SUPERINTENDANT'S OFFICE – DAY

Fortunately CARL managed to phone ROWENA when he was
arrested and she arrives with Hobart's best solicitor at this time.
ROWENA has her arm around ALEX as the immaculately
dressed SOLICITOR talks with the SUPERINTENDANT. FROM
ALEX'S POV, the non verbal inaudible discussion favours him.
His SOLICITOR approaches him.

MR JENKINS

...and verballing is no Lay down Mazaire for
police these days and you've clearly been a
victim here. I can promise you all charges
will be dropped...apart from the incident at
the school. It's tricky.

ALEX looks crestfallen.

ALEX

But I had to use force - to save that boy from
possible death maybe. Hospital, anyway – so
does that mean?

JENKINS
I know that but they'll coerce you into
resigning. I'm sorry.

ON ALEX FROM ROWENA'S POV. HE'S DEVASTATED.

ROWENA
But..it could be worse? You said you were
only going to stay till Christmas.

ALEX
Something good happened to me there.
Changed my life and mind. I wanted to leave
in my own time.

#132 INT. ALEX'S HOME – DAY

ROWENA (READING FROM
NEWSPAPER)
My God but this is biased! They're calling
you a thug who should be permanently
black- balled from the profession.

ROWENA
I'd happily move interstate with you.

ALEX(THE STORY WOUNDS HIM)
That's not an option for me right now.

When she raises her eyebrows he answers.
I've been thinking since my arrest..there are
things I still have to tell you. They're big. But
I'm hoping, you may think enough of me to
cope..

He's got her attention now but changes the subject.

141

ALEX

Also, you need to get JASON to watch those vulnerable kids..when school goes back next week. They'll need protection more than ever now.

ROWENA

Any chance you could explain those BIG THINGS before changing the subject again?

ALEX

Well, you know that I'm sick..well, probably dying is a more accurate word. I came here to Tasmania to find a plant. But no ordinary plant. It can cure me..

ROWENA

But why can't you get it from a chemist or Pharmaceutical Company?

ALEX

It's the world's rarest plant. No Drug Companies know it exists. And I suppose... I discovered it.

ROWENA

But if you did that you could be famous, and rich! Well, richer... Anyway, if it's as brilliant at fighting disease as you say, this medication should be available to everyone shouldn't it? I'm amazed though that you of all people would keep something like this a secret – and not share it. You're such a good and philanthropic man!

ALEX

But an emotionally dumb one! I always
meant to do good things with it. But I always
found it hard enough just to survive! I
needed the school - to be with people and as
a cover for me. I came here to Tasmania to
disappear and come in from the cold. I had
some trouble years ago. In America. With...!

She's in open mouthed shock. What's coming next?

ROWENA

The Police?

ALEX

I never really knew how to live my life till I
met you. I was orphaned - a street kid from
when I was young; always alone. I stole food,
clothes, books. I'm a self made kleptomaniac
pretty much.

ROWENA

But what about Humanity. The good this
plant could do?

ALEX

I never had a high opinion of 90% of
humanity. Thought most of our species
was garbage. A Virus even. But I was
only partly right. Anyway...You're back at
school Monday and I have to head for the
mountains for a few days.

She stares at him. Maybe she doesn't really know him.
Think I know the area to look for it now. It'll
save my life if I can find it. I'm asking you to
give me and us this chance? I'm asking Trust
me. Back me.

He studies her face. She submits to trust him implicitly.

#134 EXT. SALAMANCA HARBOUR MARKET. WEEKEND.
DAY

The couple is wandering in the Salamanca Markets at the docks when
ALEX is seen from the POV of a disturbed white haired old man. In
the background is a huge passenger ship moored at the dock.
CLOSE. The unhealthy and curmudgeonly man looks increasingly
vaguely familiar despite being in his 90's and having a pronounced
limp. He becomes more and more agitated and is visibly shaking to
the extent he's turning heads and distressing his wife. He tries to get
closer to ALEX and ROWENA. The old man, gradually becomes
recognizable as retired Sheriff DORFMANN. The aged couple follow
ALEX and ROWENA as best they can through the populous markets. The ex sheriff is clearly on a mission of revenge.
DORFMANN sees him close up and his mouth drops in shock
as he recognizes ALEX as only 25 years or so older than when he
last saw him. ALEX glances at him but there is no spark of rec-
ognition despite the older man almost visibly "blowing a gasket".
ALEX and ROWENA merely exchange puzzled looks and walk
away from him. DORFMANN ushers his exhausted wife into a
café so he can pursue his quarry. DISSOLVE TO
TRACKING: DORFMANN follows them along the harbour and
watches the couple enter their building and writes the address.
Worn out,he plods breathlessly back to the dock area looking like
he could have a heart attack as he makes a mobile phone call.

HARRY DORFMANN
Hello operator. Is that Langley Virginia.
Yeah, Mister ROBERT DORFMANN,
Special Ops. Thanks. Hello? Hello?
BOBBY? Yeah, Yeah we're both fine. No, it's
something else. You need to get down here
son. Remember a story I told you 'bout an
incident back in 1965 about a bunch a stuff..
And you're gonna need a team son. Now
listen carefully.

DORFFMANN pulls an old and yellowing newspaper clipping from his bum-bag featuring an identikit drawing and a barely recognizable photo of ALEX (NILS)taken in 1965. DORFF-MANN puts on thick glasses and peers at the pictures with a nasty smile. DISSOLVE TO FLASHBACK
SUPER CAMELIA U.S.FLASHBACK 1965

#135 EXT. CAMELIA AND WOODLAND. U.S.1965 – NIGHT

Back in the Deep South it's suddenly as "yesterday". NILS (ALEX) watches the pick-trucks' lights as they suddenly come to a stop 12 miles from town.

From NILS'(ALEX) POV the Kombie Van can just be discerned as being parked by the side of the road. As he silently drives a little closer he can see a struggle taking place. He squints and discerns several figures being hit and then bundled into the back seats of two of the trucks. Another figure opens the bonnet of the Kombie and does something under the raised hood before getting into the vehicle. All the vehicles now drive off for a mile before heading off the highway along a side road into dense forest.

NILS follows the lights of the trucks in his Caddy another few miles, his lights off and the engine barely audible. He opens his glove box as he drives and pulls a Browning from it checking the chamber is full, while never losing sight of the lights in front. He also pulls out a half sized baseball bat from under his seat. The trucks now turn off into an unmade winding track. After another five minutes Nils sees the trucks pull into a clearing and he turns his Caddy back the way he came, hides it in a stand of trees and runs soundlessly back, gun in hand.

In the clearing he sees one of the parked trucks has left its headlights on and he can see the "cops" are drinking again. They're drunk, violent, fingering their gun triggers while watching the three students kneeling over an old disused mine shaft. One of the Deputies has to pee. He walks thirty metres away from the others and Nils is suddenly behind him and knocks him senseless with the wooden bat. In fifteen more seconds Nils is behind one of the trucks, his deadly aim trained on the SHERIFF.

FROM Nils POV the kids are on their knees sobbing in terror. DORFMANN sways unsteadily for an instant as he cocks his weapon. At this instant Nils fires two deadly accurate shots and fells the Sheriff with a thigh shot and a Deputy with a shoulder shot. The other Deputy and the mechanic race off into the woods in terror.

> ### NILS
> Get up guys. It's me, NILS. Don't give up
> on me now. I'm getting you out of this but
> you have to run like you've never run before
> and hang tough. Come on, you can do it you
> guys!

They're whimpering as they follow him as fast as they can. NILS runs past the Sheriff writhing in pain, and then stops, returns and kicks him in the testicles for good measure, making him scream even louder. He pumps bullets into the tyres and grabs the Sheriff's two way radio as well.

SHERIFF (SCREAMING)
I'll kill you! I'll kill you, you fuck!

NILS
Not if I kill you first NUMBNUTS.

SHERIFF (APOPLECTIC)
I'll hunt you to the ends of the Earth. You'll run but you can't hide. You Fucker! You Fucker...

NILS leads the youngsters at desperate speed back to his car. He hits the accelerator and they race back up track, hit the main road and speed off into the night towards the northern highway. He dons night vision glasses and keeps the lights off, taking a number of detours when he sees lights in the rear view mirror. He's a special talent.

#136 MEMPHIS AIRPORT DAY

Early the following morning he buys them tickets at Memphis airport and gets them on the plane to New York.

> ### LORETTA
> I don't know what to say NILS. We were
> lost...dead and buried till you came. That
> Redneck would have.. I can't believe it..

She's traumatized and fights more sobbing.

> ### CHARLIE
> Yeah Man. You're the best. You saved our
> asses.

> ### JOHN
> We can never repay you man. I still
> don't understand why we don't go to the
> Montgomery police and get that mother-
> fucker. He'd do serious time..!

> ### NILS
> Things don't operate like that down here.
> I have to leave this country today. So, lead
> good lives you guys: stay north of the Mason
> Dixon Line and stay safe, okay?

They hug him before he disappears in the airport crowd. DISSOLVE TO PRESENT
SUPER: PRESENT DAY 2027

#137 INT. HOBART AIRPORT.MORNING.PRESENT DAY

HARRY DORFFMANN stands in the airport lounge glancing at

an old INTERPOL picture and dossier on ALEX as he half watches a big plane land.

#138 EXT. HOBART AIRPORT. DAY

HARRY DORFMANN, accompanied by his son, BOBBY exit the airport and head for two unmarked police cars. BOBBY's a younger version of his father, but bigger, stronger, smarter and more dangerous.

He is accompanied by two other "SPOOKS" – one an Australian ASIO operative who looks as if he's read too many Robert Ludlum thrillers, judging by his trench coat and posturing. The ubiquitous detective Snowden gets out of one of the cars and introduces himself to the DORFMANNS before the cars drive off. DISSOLVE TO

#139 INT. HOTEL GRAND EXCELSIOR HOBART - NIGHT.

CLOSE ON A COMPUTER SCREEN. BOBBY DORFMANN is writing the name "DR J JENS and the names "The ROMSVELDT INSTITUTE" and "INTERPOL" can be discerned. He's writing fast - a man on a mission.

#140 EXT. SALAMANCA HOBART – DAY

ALEX enters the WILDERNESS Shop and makes several purchases in preparation for another mountain trip.
When he emerges from the shop carrying some heavy bags he's vigilant when he notices a man he saw earlier and is now visibly convinced he's being followed. On his way home he loses his two pursuers and enters an electronics shop.

#141 INT. ALEX'S APARTMENT - DAY.

He's bought three closed circuit televisions and sets them up in three parts inside and outside the apartment. He also places some bugging devices around the unit. His rucksack packed and dressed for trekking he takes a peek through the tiny gap in the drawn curtains at the nearby harbour walkway and sees one of the men he saw at the docks, reading a newspaper. It's proof positive.

#142 EXT. HOBART AND MOUNTAIN DRIVE – DAY

From the Australian Spook's POV ALEX drives out of the "secure" underground garage and heads for the highway to the mountains. The Spook makes two Mobile phone calls. SEVERAL DISSOLVES SHOW ALEX driving out of the city and into the mountains. He casts periodic glances over his shoulder and sees a standard grey sedan behind him following.
When he passes through a country town he notices it drop off but another standard family sedan in blue takes its place and decides to risk a Mobile call to ROWENA at school

#143 INT. CLASSROOM WICKLOW – DAY
ROWENA's teaching a senior class.

ROWENA
.. therefore MAYELLA EWELL, Boo
Radley and Tom Robinson parallel the
mockingbirds Atticus Finch says should
never be harmed - they are the vulnerable
and harmless victims of MAYCOMB
"society's" hypocrisy and its dramatically
ironic and dangerous double standards ....
(muttering half to herself) a little bit like this
country of ours these days you might say..

Suddenly the Mobile goes off.

GENEVIEVE
That's a NO No Miss JAMES. Remember the
no Mobiles rule! The only Mobile allowed
here is the Mobile Alabama in this novel.

ROWENA
Sorry. Could you all write a thumbnail
assessment of how Atticus Finch taught his
kids about empathy. I'll just be a moment.

#144 INT/EXT. JUMP CUT FROM CLASSROOM TO CAR

ALEX
ROWIE - I'm so sorry. I knew it was a
mistake.

CLOSE ON ROWENA. She thinks the worst.

ALEX
The cops, ASIO and the CIA are after
me. Probably also the Salvation Army the
way my luck's going. I can't return to the
apartment. I'm going to have to go to ground
for a while. I know you don't understand. I'm
not a bad criminal, I promise you. I love you.
Contact you soon.

The Mobile's suddenly out of range.

ROWENA
ALEX, ALEX I have to t..

FADE TO BLACK:

#145 EXT. MOUNTAIN FOREST TRAIL – DAY

ALEX drives off the highway and follows several Ranger Fire Trails up and into the wilderness. He hides the car and exits with a backpack and starts jogging slowly into the deepening forest looking dangerously ill.
MOVING - As ALEX treks deeper into the dark heart of the alpine forest he soon realizes that someone expert is following him.
CUT TO – BOBBY DORFMANN's a good athlete and jogging well along another trail, tracking him. He's clearly a worthy adversary.
PAN TO - ALEX glimpses his pursuer through binoculars about a mile distant and now really pushes himself to a superhuman effort. He's terribly sick but his face reveals his life is in the balance. He sustains a loping run for maybe five miles despite stopping periodically to dry reach or cough blood. DISSOLVE TO

#146 EXT.MOUNTAIN FOREST.DUSK

He loses his fastest pursuer for about five hours and enters a wilder part of this great forest. Shortly after, he stumbles into a small dell not dissimilar to the ones in Mesopotamia and Alabama and when he slumps down amongst the greenery in fatigue, he is suddenly elated when he spots another tiny island in a brook. He examines it and smells it and smiles joyfully before wolfing down a mouthful of the leaves with a mouthful from the brook. He hermetically seals the remaining leaves in a jar he takes from his rucksack.
He's elated and now shaves off his beard and hides his tracks expertly before doubling back for more an hour before heading in a different direction. A SERIES OF DISSOLVES
He's visibly regaining some of his vitality and running better. He keeps up a north easterly direction for several hours then sets his

watch alarm for four hours and lies down in a thermal blanket to sleep. It's early morning when he wakes and sets off jogging again wearing night glasses.

#147 EXT. TASMANIAN FOREST – DAY

MLS. From a distance he's running very fast. A zooming POV shows him once more "reborn" and in his prime as he runs fast under canopies of towering conifers. He coughs several times but there's no longer any blood. In his joy though he drops his guard again when he emerges from this majestic wood, and carelessly sprints out onto a forest fire trail.

#148 EXT. TASMANIAN FOREST FIRE TRAIL – DAY

Even though it is a remote place, the police have a dragnet out to catch him and there's an unmarked police car twenty metres away and an officer points a gun at him while getting out of the car. He trains it on Alex, who reluctantly surrenders.

> ### POLICEMAN KERRY SPENCER
> Stay where you are mate. Hands in the Air!
> Hey, KEN, could you bring me the photo of
> that Wanted bloke. This isn't him is it?

HARRY doesn't get out of the car but looks at the photo.

> ### OFFICER KEN STACK (YELLING)
> No way! The guy we're looking is grey
> bearded heavier and 25 years older. More!

The other cop puts his gun back in its holster and is about to let ALEX go, when forty metres away a large well built running man bursts out of the bush onto the unmade road. They all stare at him in surprise. As he strides towards them, he's breathing heavily.

> ### BOBBY DORFMAN (SUSPICIOUS)
> Where'd do you come from Buddy? I've been
> chasing someone. You're not him though. Do
> you have some I.D on you? What's your name?

ALEX:
GEOFF EDMUND. Why, what's up?

BOBBY DORFMANN
And what were you doing in there?

ALEX
I'm a freelance photographer taking pictures
for an Australian Geographic story on
Tasmanian Devils.

A friend of mine reckons the brain tumours
they're getting are from Human Pappaloma
virus – you know, from eating tampons left
by eco-tourists who aren't burying 'em deep

enough. So I'm, you know, doing an
investigative story with heaps of pictures
and..

He shows DORFFMAN his SLR. It's a convincing spiel.

DORFMANN
Er, yeah! Well that all sounds, er, fascinating
feller. You seem to be on the level buddy, but
right now we're seeking a very important
fugitive, so, reluctant as I am to do it, I'm
gonna have to ask you to go with these
Hobart Officers back to the central station.
This is a highly important exercise and
we're gonna have to take DNA samples and
fingerprints of all people of ..interest.

ALEX (UNFAZED)
I'm supposed to catch the Sydney plane
tonight..is that still a possibility?

DORFMANN
Sure, but I can't promise anything. I'll See
what I can do.

#149 INT. HOBART POLICE STATION – DAY

Inside the station one recognizes Alex from his last visit. He is far
too youthful. Initially he's just a suspect and sits in a small room
getting his finger prints taken and DNA tested. He's looking for
any chance to escape.
ALEX watches the cops go through the formalities of paperwork
and taking the samples. There are too many cops around. He
awaits the imminent "fire-storm".

#150 INT.POLICE STATION RECEPTION AREA. DAY

When BOBBY arrives with his father, the son nods to ALEX as
he walks past him. DORFMANN senior is enjoying himself in
the limelight as he limps into the reception area. ALEX reads a
newspaper so neither sees the other when the DORFMANNS
pass him. ALEX walks into the TV room, casually watched by
a nubile young female cop, where he tries to use the Mobile,
but the battery's dead.

#151 INT. ALEX AND ROWENA'S APARTMENT -
NIGHT.

ROWENA's alone in the lounge, looking distressed and flick-
ing through ALEX's "library". She finds a very old Botany book
wrapped in silk among his things and among the pages she
comes upon ALEX's miniature painting and three very old
faded photographs that snatch her breath away.
CLOSE - She sits sipping wine when she recovers from her
initial shock, and studies each picture carefully with a magnifying glass. The first and oldest is the miniature painting of
ALEX when he was known as NILS, posing with his Danish
family in 1819.
The second a faded 1840's Daguerre-otype of NILS in For-

eign Legion uniform standing outside a dangerous looking cantina with two fierce Mescalero APACHES in Mexico; in the third picture, young well-to-do NILS poses with British Prime Minister Lord Asquith at a 1913 violin recital. Standing close by is ELIZABETH (then unknown to NILS). ROWENA's astonished by ELIZABETH, as there's an uncanny resemblance between them. In the final photo, taken in a 1930's Louisiana Jitney joint, NILS, saxophone in hand, stands on a stage with a sultry black woman to an African American crowd while a black jazz band plays in the background.

> ## ROWENA (ALOUD)
> Oh ALEX. What a madman's life you've led. No wonder you're such an eccentric mess! What human being could survive all this?

She now carefully replaces the pictures back in the book. CUT TO:

#152 INT. GREENWOOD FAMILY'S HOUSE.

The youth is alone in his room. He's gaunt and lost and looking at a photo of him as a youngster on a holiday in the mountains with his mum and dad. They're rugged up like Antarctic explorers and in the background are bluffs and snowdrifts. It shows they were once a happy family. He gets off his bed and walks to a map of the mountains and makes a coloured texta cross at Cradle Mountain and then looks back at the photo. ON HIS FACE in the mirror. He looks into the abyss of it and then closer on his face and the tears well in his eyes and his mouth quivers and his shoulders convulse.

#153 INT. HOBART POLICE STATION – NIGHT

MOVING THROUGH THE STATION CORRIDORS eight sets of striding suited and blue uniformed legs, the stomp of black shoes and one set of gym shoes on the wooden floor.
FROM THE POV of a handful or cops on night duty and working

at desks, BOBBY DORFMANN, two Spooks and seven cops of varying rank are almost marching towards the Television room. Several startled desk cops look out their doors at the heavyweight group wondering what the heck is going on.

#154 INT. TELEVISION ROOM. POLICE STATION. NIGHT.

FROM ALEX'S POV the TV room door is suddenly flung open and BOBBY enters the room and towers over him slumped in any easy chair as he is. SNOWDEN stands behind the American, gloating. They all stare at ALEX as if he's an alien.

DORFFMAN
AL... NILS SALSTROM... I had intended arresting you for the suspected murder of local teacher ALEX SELKIRK, but...and I can't believe I'm actually saying this, the DNA results and finger- printing we have carried out prove conclusively that you and he are one and the same person. You have been wanted by

Interpol and the United States C.I.A since 1965 for the malicious and felonious wounding of three police officers from the County of Camellia Alabama in October 1965. .and also on charges of sedition and affray brought against you in your absence by the Scotland Yard as of August 2 1914...

ALEX looks to a slightly built woman with mousy hair who is taking notes throughout. He notices a small Police media Unit sticker on her coat lapel and sighs in pained resignation.

DORFFMAN
But given the circumstances and the years in between, the British charge is obviously void. Is there anything you wish to say or ask at this point Mr SALSTROM?

ALEX
Yeah, would a conjugal visit and a Marinara
Pizza with anchovies be out of the question?

DORFMANN
You're digging your own grave now buddy.

ALEX/NILS
My own grave? That'll be a nice change.

#155 DORFMANN SHAKES HIS HEAD AT HIM AS IF TO
SAY "YOU'RE A WISE GUY IDIOT" AND THEN MAKES A
FACE TO THE OTHER

suited spooks as if to say "Let's make this guy's life
a nightmare". DISSOLVE TO:

#156 INT. PRISON CELL POLICE HEADQUARTERS DAY/
NIGHT

ALEX is incarcerated and being watched around the clock by two
officers. One of them passes him some world newspapers through
the bars and grins encouragingly.

YOUNG COP (CHEERFUL, DECENT)
I wouldn't be so depressed if I were you
mate. You're gonna make a motsa on JIMMY
FALLON and ELLEN DE GENERES.

Your stuff'll put that Viagra outta business.
And don't forget all those Hollywood
babes looking for a sugar daddy. I bet the
KARDASHIAN sisters and SCARLET
JOHANNSON wouldn't have been with a
200 year old yet.

He laughs out loud as ALEX regards him blankly and then studies the newspaper before and after pictures of himself and other pictures of him going back to a concert he gave in Budapest in 1890s. The headlines around the world are sensational and talk of medical miracles and cures for everything from cancer to PARKINSON's in a miraculous newly discovered plant.

ALEX gazes from a second storey-window at a swarm of international Paparazzi that's descended on Hobart city and many are camped across the boulevard and in the park opposite. Three uniformed officers now arrive and escort him along a corridor to a private room.

#157 INT. INTERROGATION ROOM. HOBART GAOL – DUSK

DORFMANN and Australian Spooks await him, scrutinizing his every move. ALEX sits down in a seat opposite DORFMANN, who is seated in a higher chair behind an imposing leather desk

DORFFMANN

So, it's come to this - a frickin Media Circus. It's now time for you to disappear for a while SALSTROM. Your Government has approved your extradition to MARYLAND where you'll be tried before undergoing some...erm, scientific tests..

ALEX glances darkly at him and the other spooks.

I know this is all very sudden, but we're flying out of Hobart tonight. Shortly we'll take you to your home for half an hour..give you time to pack a small case of essentials... and say good bye to your partner. And I do mean "good bye". We've been checking out your flat and will have another last look before departing there by 0700 tonight. Are we clear?

ALEX

As Clingwrap!

#158 INT. ALEX/NILS' UNIT – NIGHT

A SERIES OF DISSOLVES, QUICK CUTS AND QUICK PANS

The Unit is swarming with Police and Spooks combing every "nook and cranny". ALEX is only given a few minutes to be close with ROWENA and even then DORFMANN is eaves-dropping. ALEX is on edge as he takes in all that is happening while packing a small suitcase. ROWENA mouths "I love you" to him across the room. A tall Spook places handcuffs on the dining room table.

DORFMANN and the scientist interview ALEX in the lounge while the others go through all of their belongings, riffle through books and so on. At this moment SNOWDEN arrives with a senior ASIO rep with further extradition paper work for the Spooks to fill out.

PHIL (ASIO OFFICER)
I'm sorry for the glitch Mr DORFMANN.
Just protocol. We changed your flight tickets
tonight for the 9PM flight.

The American's really annoyed. SNOWDEN's not just a bully, but an ambitious show- pony. This is his moment in the sun. He approaches ALEX, who stands in a hostile way. SNOWDEN's wary around ALEX. He nods at ROWENA, or rather, at her breasts. She pulls her cardigan up tightly and one of the younger Cops sees this and grins.

ALEX and BOBBY size each other up and the American's face recognizes he is potentially dangerous. ALEX notes SNOWDEN clearly defers to the Spook.

SNOWDEN
Uh, Mr Dorfm..er I should tell you now that
I suspect the prisoner of m..

Dorfmann shuts him up with a withering look. Alex gives Rowena an articulate look. She clearly knows he plans to escape. Snowden tries to throw his weight around.

SNOWDEN

This is no time to get cute with your
"BOILER" girlfriend SELKIRK or
SALSTROM or whatever your real name is.
Capiche?

ALEX clenches his fists in fury at Snowden's usage of this nasty
"boiled old chook" epithet referring to ROWENA's age. he also
visibly remembers Snowden using the word "capiche"

ALEX

Step outside with me now you baboon. I dare
you. You are dead set the worst excuse for
a Lawman...since Sergeant PLOD, in that
kids' book "NODDY". I would, however, like
to take this opportunity to commend you
on your uncharacteristically good work in
turning HARLEY GREENWOOD..or was
it BURLEY GREENWOOD...into fish food
after organizing for him to be involuntarily
launched off the Empress of Tasmania into
the Bass Strait briny. Yep, I know for a fact
you sent him to DAVY JONES's locker
Turdface "flatfoot" (pinching Harley's words
to Snowden).

Must be the most worthwhile thing you've
done since you were a piglet.

The American gives SNOWDEN a withering look and
SNOWDEN melts in fear, shock and utter defeat. DORFMANN
now stands to his imposing full height. He motions ALEX to follow him to the French windows near the balcony with a view of
the harbour, where they talk turkey. They speak to each other in
low voices watched closely by all the others..

DORFFMANN

You're in a world of Shit SALSTROM.You do
realize that?

161

ALEX

It's always been a Shitty World so that goes
without saying. Not a smart move using that
micro-cephalic Cop in there to stir me. It
doesn't engender cooperative leanings in me
you realize.

They glance at SNOWDEN simultaneously.

DORFFMANN

That cluster-fuck is finished. And he's the
least of your worries Peckerwood. Believe
me: If you want to avoid becoming a human
pin cushion with the brain capacity and
social life of a battery chicken ..you'd

DORFAMAN

better start playing ball as of ..Yesterday! Ever
heard of the ROMSVELDT Clinic, Boy Scout?

ALEX glares at him for a second, and DORFMANN inadvertent-
ly shows a frisson of fear.

DORFMANN

You're no fool, I'll give you that. And you
must know what I - what WE want. You've got

something..found something very-very
special. Everyone

in the world wants what you've discovered.
That plant is priceless. America wants it and I
want it and I won't rest till I get it. Are we on
the same page?

ALEX

Is it page 1 of the Book of Revelations? You
and I both know you and YOURS would not
do the right thing by IT.

DORFFMANN
And you HAVE? Would? What great
works of philanthropy have you used
it for since you discovered it? You used
it for yourself alone and you have the
kahoneys to criticize us? You're a fucking
hypocrite.

ALEX is suddenly dumbstruck with this basic truth. He's
pale,guilt-stricken and speechless for a moment

ALEX
I - I have done some things. I always
meant to do more.. I saw many terrible
things. Saw human garbage by the
shipload killing their own-kind over 200
years. I looked..was always looking, have
been looking for ways. I did..I have.

He's suddenly angry and self righteous
Anyway, we both know what YOU
would use it for DORFMANN, and how
Multinational Pharmaceutical companies
would hijack it! Only sell it to rich
bastards and destroy vast forests for it.
DORFFMANN? Now where have I heard
that name before..

DORFMANN
Try Alabama 1965 Peckerwood. My Dad was
a small town Sheriff there.

It suddenly dawns on ALEX what's happened.

ALEX
Ah! Okayyy! I'm with you now. You're the
Son of Sheriff PECKERWOOD.. I remember
him now. At the Salamanca docks

ALEX
the other day.. the angry old fart with a face
like cane toad road-kill and a bad limp..
probably a consequence of molesting too
many hoofed - farm animals as a teenager

ALEX smirks as he watches DORFMANN's face turn purple.

ALEX
Su-re. It's all coming back to me. Your Dad
was, make that IS a..

DORFMANN
You shot him you yellow BASTARD. It's get-
even time.

ALEX
..was an evil MURDERER: a Herpes wart!
He would've killed three innocent young
people in cold blood if I hadn't stopped
him. So what I did is called Justice, you
Fascist creep. No matter where you come
from! Your old man is the kind of low life
I was including in that "human garbage"
comment, BOY!

DORFFMANN (RAISES HIS FISTS)
Why you arrogant MOTHERFU......

ALEX
Why do people keep calling me arrogant!

DORFMANN explodes and looks set to strike ALEX but his sur-
vival instinct and a nearby Spook cool the moment.

SPOOK PATRICK
Mr DORFFMANN, I need you to look at

these notes for a minute. Please.

ALEX is ordered to sit down while the five cops now start lifting his carpets and "going to town" on the place.

ALEX (PAINED LOOK)
Hey, DORFMANN. Any chance of relieving myself in my own toilet. While I still own one?

DORFMANN
Maybe. SNOWDEN, you and CHIP go and check the latrine before this douche bag uses it. Check it thoroughly.

They do but find nothing untoward.

CHIP
All clear Sir. The only escape route's down the cistern.

DORFMANN picks up the handcuffs to cuff him but the ASIO man nods disapproval and DORFMANN okays it. Two burly policemen follow ALEX to his bedroom toilet. It's quite a stout door and ALEX silently locks it. Inside, he starts making some loud coughing noises and bowel- straining noises while climbing silently onto the toilet seat. He removes the false ceiling and hauls himself into the hidden escape hatch above it. In seconds he's covered the hole over again and in the air duct.

#160 INT/EXT. APARTMENT BLOCK HOBART – NIGHT

In an instant he's snaking along the surface of the narrow air duct. Minutes later he escapes into the main air duct of the complex. TRACKING as he crawls along this narrow duct and when he peers through an air vent can clearly see a powerful looking ASIO officer standing guard outside his door, twenty metres away. He crawls along further and suddenly hears one of the spooks yell out to the others and they come running into his bedroom. ALEX hears them pounding on his toilet door as he soundlessly drops

three metres to land in a stairwell at another level in the building.
CUT TO:

#161 EXT. CHANNEL HIGHWAY NEAR HOBART - NIGHT.

It's night on the highway to the mountains. The cars are moving
fast. In the headlights of a truck a BOY in an anorak with a small
backpack is hitch-hiking.
From the POV of car slowing down to pick up the youth,
DAMIEN can be seen limping towards the passenger door.

#162 INT. ALEX'S UNIT - NIGHT.

The Cops and Feds break down the toilet door and find him gone.
DORFMANN goes ballistic.

> ## DORFFMAN
> You BETTER catch that Sonuvabitch Your
> Goddam jobs depend on it! Jesus H. Christ!
> How did you sorry arsed prophylactics ever
> get jobs with The Firm?

SNOWDEN's hurrying towards the stairwell but glances sheep-
ishly at DORFFMANN as he punches a hole in a wall.

> ## DORFMANN
> Consider yourself on duty till the morning
> - till we catch him SNOWDEN. After that
> we'll look into his accusation against you.

SNOWDEN's white faced.

#163 INT.ALEX'S BUILDING. NIGHT.

ALEX looks up towards the uproar upstairs as he sprints down
basement stairs and out through the underground security
car park with them in hot pursuit running in every direction
throughout the building yelling to each other on their mobiles.

#164 EXT. HOBART HARBOUR – NIGHT

They're running from the apartment block but ALEX is already sprinting along one of the outer harbour piers. Cops and Spooks are racing towards the docks on foot or speeding in cars. Some of the harbour and marina is ill lit in places and the night overcast. The lights of moored boats and smaller craft complement the revolving big yellow light on the harbour gate. Alex pauses, looking for the best escape route. PAN POV OF THE HARBOUR. COPS have cut his options. He's got no choice and swims between several sailing boats, hiding in their shadows. CLOSE ON his face - the waters are dangerously icy.

#165 EXT. HOBART HARBOUR – NIGHT

Three solid Policemen are just visible under a pier lamp at an isolated part of the harbour. They're even shivering in their coats while directing powerful torches on the water. ALEX shelters in the water underneath them. An unmarked Police car pulls up. Snowden gets out.

SNOWDEN (HE'S SHAKING IN FEAR)

Listen you blokes. Don't hesitate with this Perp. He's dangerous and probably armed. The Yanks want him alive but you'll get no grief from me if you pop him. Okay?

They all grunt acknowledgement as he departs.

CONSTABLE 1

How the Hell did that haemorrhoid suppository make lieutenant? No wonder the Force's getting such a bagging in the media! Did he Really just call the fugitive a Perp? As in perpetrator.. and say it's okay to POP him? I reckon SNOWDEN's learned all his policing protocols watching the bloody SOPRANOS.

The others have a chuckle.

167

CONSTABLE 2.
He might have a bit of a point though JOE
- apart from the one at the top of his head.
Salstrom gave three of our guys a hiding in
the cells.

Did he seem shit scared to anyone else but
me? Hell it's cold! The bloke's obviously not
around here. I think we ought to split up
and meet around the other side near the fish
restaurant over there. All agreed say "aye".
The ayes have it.

They now head off in the opposite direction.

#166 EXT. HOBART HARBOUR AND DOCKS - LATE DAY.

ALEX has no choice and swims an open thirty metres to a bigger
vessel. Suddenly a large creature in the water buffets him. He is
momentarily terrified until a huge sea lion surfaces and brushes
against him in a playful fashion.

ALEX
Thank Christ, not a shark! But I just know
you'll want to bite me anyway.

A nearby Spook has heard the noise and runs to the dock edge waving a flashlight and pointing a gun. ALEX dives as a light strafes the
water catching the beautiful animal in a startled pose. Others arrive
and the creature plays up to the amusement of one of the cops.
ALEX emerges drags himself out of the harbour 50 metres distant
and crawls onto a ledge under one of the pylons supporting the
wooden dock. He's getting hypothermia. Nearby, cops and Spooks
huddle and parlay outside a popular local fish and chip shop, as a
wind mounts.

#167 EXT/INT. BATTERY POINT – NIGHT

Shortly, ALEX is running slowly through the rabbit warren of streets of National Heritage precinct Battery Point. He stumbles along a footpath in exhaustion and sees what looks like an empty cottage. He breaks in by pulling off his saturated jumper and punching through a window with it. Once inside he removes his saturated clothing and switches on a radiator. He finds clothes and shoes that fit but his body is still convulsing from the shock he's endured. He now sights the phone.

> ### ALEX
> Hello? JASON it's ALEX...erm NILS. I don't want to, bother you, but I'm desperate and on the run. I can't call Rowena - her line will be tapped. And for what it's worth, I have never done anything evil or bad...except where it was deserved. I tried to do good. No matter what THEY say..

> ### JASON
> You don't have to convince me. I'm there for you ALEX.
>
> And I'm asking your forgiveness. I've been a moron and paid the price. And you warned me. Helped me too. I'll find ROWIE ..and we'll get you out of this mess.

#168 EXT. HERITAGE SUBURB BATTERY POINT. NIGHT.

DISSOLVES: Minutes later ALEX is running furtively up side streets and alleys. After a few miles he looks up a deserted street he spies a hedge enclosed football field and old school. He's about to run again but instinctively hides behind a parked car when he hears a slow moving car approaching. From his POV two Spooks cruise slowly past his cover.

#169 EXT. TREE FRINGED SCHOOL OVAL.

A sedan with only it's tail light on drives into the football ground entrance. ALEX hurries from the trees and jumps into JASON's car. ROWENA's there and hugs him.

ALEX (SHIVERING)

Th..thank goodness! I'm fighting the onset of hypothermia..

#170 INT. JASON'S CBD UNIT.EARLY MORNING

Later they sit drinking coffee in his kitchen. ALEX is now wearing a big jacket but still shivering.

ALEX

I've been lucky so far tonight. But it's D Day now. SNOWDEN wants me dead and the Spooks will take me to Virginia and kill me forensically cell-by-cell. I thought..maybe head for New Zealand, lay low for a few months. After that, maybe the sub continent? I don't expect you to follow me ROWIE?

ROWENA

Of course I will. But.. .. something awful's happened to one of your students..

ALEX intuitively knows who it is

JASON

Yeah it's that poor kid DAMIEN. He went missing late last yesterday arvo. But he's not your responsibility ALEX..er NILS.

ALEX

Children are everyone's responsibility

ROWENA

SALLY and GRETEL came to me yesterday. They're in a bad way. Both think he's gone into the mountains somewhere to..

> ### ALEX
> To... top himself? I think they're right. He needed protection from that evil stuff. I blame myself. How long ago? We have to save him.

> ### ROWENA
> If we speak to his mother. The girls think he might have gone to Cradle Mountain. It's the last holiday their family had before his dad died.

> ### ALEX
> There's no time to lose. Let's check his room and with his mum – if nothing, we try the mountain. Did you try the bus depot?

> ### ROWENA
> It was closed. Let's go..

CUT TO:
#171 EXT. HOBART STREET – NIGHT
They pull up at a distance from the GREENWOOD home. A few of the street lights are out. ALEX gets out silently and checks the street for a stake out.

#172 INT. DAMIEN'S HOUSE – NIGHT

DAMIEN'S MOTHER KAREN weeps softly as she shows them to her son's room.
CLOSE ON ROWENA - She finds family photos strewn across the bed and notices the map on the wall. Peering close she spies two tiny red crosses marked on it indicating a hut and the summit of CRADLE MOUNTAIN. She calls ALEX.

> ### ROWENA

> The girls were right. He's gone to the
> mountain. He must have hitched. Mum said
> she last saw him at 6:00 last night.

She tears down the poster and stuffs it under DAMIEN'S blankets
and heads back into the kitchen.
        DAMIEN'S MOTHER FROM ROWENA'S POV

KAREN GREENWOOD (WEEPING)
> He's such a terrific kid. He was going great
> guns until

> those Boys bashed him. How can such things
> happen? What's wrong with people today?.
> Please find him. Please help him Mr SALST..
> um SELKIRK. Um..I forgot - I called the
> police just before you arrived.

Alarmed, they head for the door as she hands ALEX a piece of
paper.

KAREN GREENWOOD
> You might want this too. It's his Mobile
> Phone number.

#173 EXT. CITY AND COUNTRY ROADS - MID MORNING.

The three immediately drive off at a legal speed, and head for
mountains. SEVERAL DISSOLVES
They drive through climbing roads that dissect dark forests. They
climb ever higher into the mountains..
As they approach the mountain it's late afternoon and a light rain
falls.

#174 EXT. CRADLE MOUNTAIN AREA - LATE AFTER-
NOON

A series of DISSOLVES. They cover untold miles in their search...
They find a deserted hut in the high area and discover a half-eat-

en chocolate bar on a table.

They look worn out as the struggle along wild trails through the deep forest.

ON ALEX as the late afternoon and the sky darkens.

> ## ALEX
> Front's moving in. It'll maybe bring snow.
> We'd better really move fast. Faster.
>
> Poor little bastard. I should have protected
> him properly..

> ## ROWENA
> No one could have protected him every
> minute. JASON and I tried hard too.
> Darling,
>
> there's no right time to tell you, but yesterday
> I found out..that I'm pregnant.

JASON glances at them in the driver mirror, smiling. ALEX is flummoxed, ecstatic, stunned, and hugs her joyfulLY despite the situation.

> ## JASON
> Way to go. That's amazing ROWENA! I
> didn't think after 48.... I mean, terrific!

> ## ALEX (LAUGHING BITTERLY)
> But that's absolutely impossibly wonderful!
> A child - a child and family, now, for me on
> this mystical island at the end of the Earth.
> God's perfect timing at last! Something
> brilliant in my interminable stupid life!

The weather's worsening as he hugs her and they head up the overgrown track once more.

#175 EXT. TRACK TO CRADLE MOUNTAIN SUMMIT – DUSK

The snow's stopped falling as they follow the steeply rising mountain track that slices its way up the mountain pass. They've got strong torches for the darkness is growing.

> ALEX
>
> Rowena...you and Jason follow as fast as you can. I'm going to run it..

> JASON
>
> I can keep up..ROWENA can follow at her own..

But ALEX has gone. He's already disappearing round a bend up ahead in the gloaming.
MONTAGE: ALEX searches the heights, jogging across the rough terrain. ROWENA and JASON'S torches lead them to the summit.

#176 EXT. MOUNTAIN SUMMIT – DUSK

They all reconnect. Once they duck down into a rock formation as they hear the whirr of a distant helicopter.

> ALEX
>
> Faen! That's shortened the odds! They know where I am. We've got to go faster. Spread out. Keep trying your Mobiles. We might get lucky!

In the wilderness wandering by a terrible escarpment, ALEX hears something. The faintest beeping noise - it's DAMIEN's Mobile battery winding down. ALEX waves his torch and yells at the top his lungs:

> ALEX
>
> Over here! Hurry.

DAMIEN's Mobile beeps its last and is carried in the wind. They're ecstatic when they discover the stricken boy. He's semi-conscious and trapped on a ledge more than two metres below a cliff top echoing ALEX's "delivery" from the Bandits early in the story.

JASON
Is he alive? Hell yeah, his chest's moving. But the ledge's unstable. It won't hold...

ALEX(HE'S MADE HIS DECISION)
Yes, it will. Lower me over.

ROWENA's fearful and uncertain. He hugs her, pats her stomach and hands her a letter. He gives each of them a small sachet of the leaves before lowering himself over the cliff's edge with JASON'S help.

ALEX
In case I don't..erm, that letter explains all.
ROWENA, know in your heart my hours
with you were the very best of my times. Eat
these leaves and berries and rekindle your
youth, but remember ... youth without
wisdom is a poisoned Chalice. Look out for
her Jason. And don't waste another precious
second of your lives. (Looking at her) A baby
for us! A family, at the end of days! But, a
family just the same...

He stops talking as he prepares to drop another two feet past
his fully stretched height. It's a near- impossible task but he
somehow does it. The ledge starts to crumble as he lands: it's
about to give way.

ROWENA (CRYING SOFTLY)
I never truly loved till I loved you..

With a tremendous show of strength he lifts DAMIEN and throws his prostrate body up towards JASON'S outstretched arms. JASON grabs him and lays his body on the grass.

He crawls to the ledge again and reaches down for ALEX, who's trying to get purchase on a piece of rock near the top. Almost simultaneously the crumbling ledge gives way. He looks up at the tearful ROWENA, strength as tears well in his eyes.

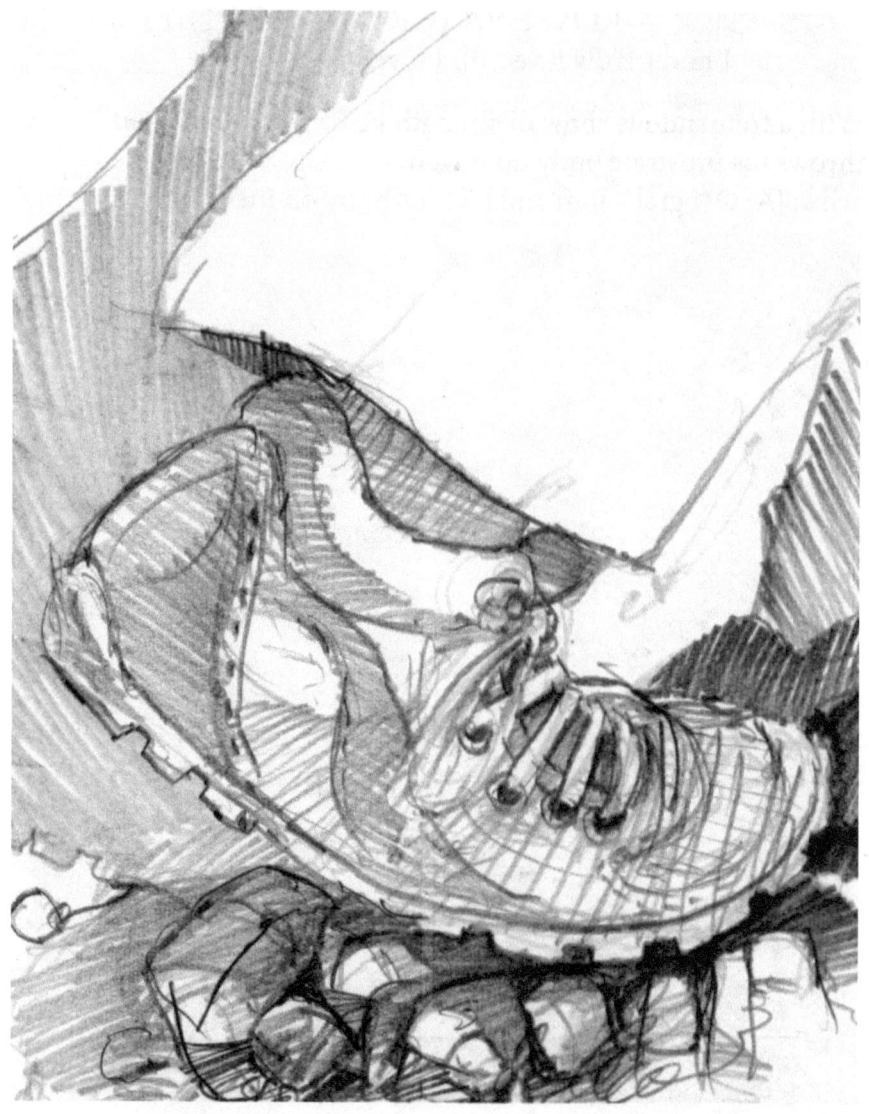

ALEX
Jeg hedder.. NILS SALSTROM. I lived my
life. I loved and was loved ... Enough!!

JASON'S grip suddenly fails him and their fingers break away as
ALEX starts to plummet soundlessly two thousand metres to his
death ROWENA's sobbing and screaming after him. JASON turns
his face away.

179

#177 EXT. CLIFF TOP AND CLIFF WALL – DUSK

A SERIES OF DISSOLVES
His fall is seen in torturously slow motion and the screen splits in two on one side from his POV he watches the "shrinking" frozen faces of his distraught friends on the cliff's edge as they watch his fall. THE SOUND OF A PIANIST PLAYING CHOPIN STARTS TO RISE IN VOLUME.

#178 EXT. THE SCANDINAVIAN GARDEN.

Split screen: on one side his friends watch his fall in hypnotic hor-ror; on the other he sees himself as the little boy in the garden again sitting in the chair. He rises and turns to face his family on the stoop, and as he walks towards them becomes Nils the man.
In the Garden he passes people from his life and image snatches of the "transported" places from his life: the English CORPORAL LEES and the Italian musician soldier salute him as he passes; the LITTLE GIRL he saved in the orphanage and the dying girl in the London hospice he saved turn to wave and smile at him; Lady ELIZABETH looks coquettish under the boughs of a tree and blows him a kiss; the three American Civil Rights YOUTHS stand by their Kombie, nod and smile thanks at him as he seems to partly levitate several times as he walks and almost glides past; JASON and his KIDS salute him with clenched fists and grin; his STUDENTS wave to him lovingly from another corner of the Garden; and just before he reaches the steps to the veranda he looks to one side and there is ROWENA next to her daughter and grand-daughter, and holding her and ALEX's baby. There are tears in her eyes as she mouths the words "I love you". His face creases in a magical ecstatic smile of Letting Go, as he waves to her longingly and mounts the steps. He can hear his family calling his name. His family reach out for him and the image starts to fade as a phantasmagoria of faces and snatches of events from his incredible life shutter impossibly quickly before his eyes, and for these "long" stretching seconds a smile forms on his face instants before...
From the POV of the distraught ROWEAN on the cliff top, he begins to fall at real blinding speed for just moments and then his body smashes onto rocks far below. FADE TO BLACK

#179 EXT. MOUNTAIN TOP - THE LAST OF DUSK 2027

JASON hugs her as they turn away from this horror and kneel over the boy. Suddenly a helicopter is heard loud and close. Powerful lights strafe the summit. The chopper descends through a cloud bank on the plateau.
ROWEANA and JASON can see dark figures peering out of the chopper towards the cliff.

> ### JASON
> I really have to go now ROWENA. The old me died here tonight too. Okay? But we'll meet again.

She gives him her sachet of the leaves.

> ### ROWENA
> I neither need nor want these. They're a curse as well as a gift.

She gazes numbly at him for a second and he nods and kisses her cheek before rushing away into the darkness. She lays her jacket over the unconscious boy and starts sobbing again as she stares into the abyss, where she can just discern the tiny body of ALEX, spread-eagled on a massive boulder far below. ROWENA watches the wild river abruptly rise up and claim him, washing him off the rock and carrying him away into ever wilder reaches, before black night falls.

#180 EXT.MOUNTAIN TOP.NIGHT

A minute later the helicopter, lit up like a space ship lands thirty metres from the ledge, and DORFMANN and three of his team leap out onto the grass and race towards ROWENA, who is still kneeling in shock by the unconscious DAMIEN. JASON is nowhere to be seen. There is shouting and a pool of sound that ebbs and flows for a few moments before fading away and all that can be and all that can be heard in the darkness is a lonely wind.
DISSOLVE TO:

#181 EXT. CHURCH IN RICHMOND TASMANIA 2027 DAY

In a surrealist SLOWMO mourners gather by the grave-side of

two empty graves with ALEX'S/NILS' and JASON's engraved names on the headstones.
WIDE IT'S THE SAME CEMETERY NILS dreamed while fighting in Mesopotamia. Both have been presumed dead.
There are many children there as well as adults, including JASON's weeping ex-wife and their heart broken young teenaged twins and ALEX's most successful protégées and SALLY, GRETEL AND RAE-LENE who sing a moving Irish hymn as DAMIEN accompanies them on a guitar. ROWENA stands next to SIMON, proudly watching the children for a moment before the empty coffins are lowered into their graves. MOVING - At that moment ROWENA smiles as she notices a powerfully built and just recognizable "17 year old" (the 'reborn' JASON) who stands on the fringe of the MOURNERS watching his estranged WIFE fighting back tears. ROWEAN smiles to herself as he approaches them and visibly comforts them in their grief. JEN sees him too and tries to get a better look at the young man ROWENA watches. JENN's face screws up in puzzlement at who she sees. At this moment a young woman with a baby steps out of the crowd of mourners and approaches ROWEAN.

ROWENA
MARY ANNE! Oh, MARY ANNE. Oh ..Oh!
And my beautiful little LOUISE! Oh it's so
wonderful to see you again. I've missed you
so much. And now a grand- daughter..

They're both crying now and hugging

MARY-ANNE
It's so great to see you mum. You look
terrific. Radiant! I left that bastard. You were
right! As you always were! The man who just
died ..the man from here..ALEX - He rang
me. Told me you needed Me. More like we
needed you. He sent us tickets, money for
hotels and expenses: Everything! A great
guy. Said he was your friend!

MARY ANNE
He got that right! It's so sad I'll never meet
him now..

ROWENA
ALEX! A wonderful selfless man...

MARY ANNE suddenly looks at her mother in astonishment as
she notices a slight tummy bulge. ROWEAN's shrug and smile
answers her. She and her daughter embrace each other and the
toddler again and despite her grief, ROWEAN's cup of happiness
"runneth" over. DISSOLVE TO:

#182 EXT. GROUNDS OF WICKLOW – DAY

A front is moving in on the following morning, and in a dark
echo of ALEX's arrival at the school, the renewed JASON (now
looking about 17, but as powerful as any man) stands near the
Derwent staring at the school from a distance, much as ALEX
arrived: a near gale blows and heavy rain falls in sheets as he
strides athletically across the fields towards the back entrance to
the school in a clear echo of Nils' arrival there.

#183 EXT.WICKLOW GROUNDS AND BUILDINGS.DAY

The siren sounds for the start of period as he makes a short
deliberate detour and rounds an outer block and there in a piece
of "serendipity" from his POV, he encounters two of the senior
school brutes who savagely beat Damien. They're standing under
the eaves swallowing amphetamines with Coca Cola. They immediately confront JASON when they see him but have no idea who
he is. WADE, the leader, is about to shove him.

WADE
Who's this wanker then? Some fresh meat....

Suddenly JASON's a terrifying monster for a few minutes, and
belts him senseless, grabs the other student by the fingers and
bends them to almost breaking point and sticks his foot on
WADE's throat. He glares from one to the other as he speaks.

JASON(GUTTERAL ICY VOICE)
On my fucking undying oath, your rule of
terror's over here, you GONAD CANCERS!
Hurt JUST one more kid at this fucking
school in any fucking way whatsoever and
I swear you'll never walk, talk or eat right
again for the rest of your short miserable
lives. You better be fucking-well hearing me!

He's diabolical, and the prone boy rolls onto his side in agony and
grunts assent and the other manages a raspy terrified "Yes" sound
as JASON lets go and he crumples to the asphalt.

#184 INT. ADMIN OFFICE WICKLOW HIGH – DAY

As he enters the building the black clouds burst and the rain falls
in sheets as before. Jenny is at the front desk talking to Doreen,
who gives the youth a strange look of as she hands him an enrol-
ment form. JEN's nearby, recognizes him from the funeral.

JENN
I saw you at yesterday's funeral for ALEX
SALSTROM and JASON CLARKE. I seem to
half remember your face from somewhere?
Did you ever attend this school before?
Because you're strangely very familiar to me.
It's like I know you somehow. It's bizarre!

The youth awkwardly averts his gaze from her just as Doreen
heads into the Principal's office carrying documents. He looks at
JENN with love in his eyes, unsure what to say.

JASON
Yeah, I know you too Miss. I really do. Um
- is it possible I could meet you for a coffee
this afternoon at the Northern Star café? In
Elizabeth Street? Say, 4:30?
I need to tell you some things. To tell the
truth, we really need to have a long talk
Miss..I mean JENN."

She's flummoxed and stares after him in disbelief. JASON saunters towards a nearby desk in an instantly recognizable gait. It finally dawns on her and she cries out pitifully.

JEN (WHISPERING AT FIRST)
Oh my God! My God! JASON! No, it's not
possible! My JASON! It can't be you! No.......!

SCRETARY DOREEN hurries to JENN when she sees her tears.

DOREEN
What's happened Love? Did that boy do this
to you?

JENN just rushes away up the corridor, sobbing.

#185 INT/EXT. HOBART - DAY/NIGHT 2027

MONTAGE OF SHOTS - JASON is a very physically powerful young man, but this time he is clearly a life-wise and enlightened 17 year old, JASON helping fellow students with homework and sport, befriending his own children as a mentor; JASON walking in the mountains with JASON. JASON and JENN sit in a café as a temporarily secret pair but appear to have a very promising future as a couple.

#186 EXT. EMPTY SCHOOLYARD. A WINTERY SUNDAY

As from the POV of some elemental force, wind-borne and gliding through the schoolyard. A few bits of paper and leaves blow through the playground on this windswept day and the POV travels into and along the labyrinthine corridors until it reaches the Music Room. The door slowly opens and the POV "glances" around the room and zooms towards an enlarged photo on the wall accompanied by a cacophony of ghostly kids' voices and the faint echoing riffs of Alex's first lesson there - the compelling rock medley he played.
CLOSE: it's a photo portrait of ALEX. Next to it is large framed portrait photo of ROWENA holding her and ALEX'S baby, as

well as GRETEL, SALLY, DAMIEN, RAELENE, MARTY, JOAN-NA and the other, Music kids, and as well as JASON and JESS and JASON'S KIDS. It looks for all-the-world like a family portrait. As indeed it is.

The now booming but moving music echoes through the building and suddenly merges with a roaring wind song as the screen fades to black. The music is subsumed by winds and then suddenly, there's total silence.

END